TECHNICALLY MAGIC

L A MICHAELS

LML BOOKS

Cover Design by: Polyarts36
Front and back cover images by: loviiiluv
Edited by Sandra Watts
Proofed by Sandra Watts

OTHER BOOKS BY L A MICHAELS

- BETWEEN HEAVEN AND HELL
- THE INNOCENT YEARS
- I LOVE YOU, I HATE YOU, I MISS YOU
- THE YOUNGISH MARRIEDS

NOVELLAS:

- OUR PRIVATE WORLD APART

This book is dedicated to the people who have to work ten times as hard as the people around them. The people who don't have things handed to them. The people who have to wait (not so) patiently. It all works out in the long run.

FORWARD BY THE AUTHOR

Once upon a time I saw the movie version of *Annie* so many times that I question if my parents would only rent instead of buy it because we watched it so much. If I wasn't watching Annie, I would be watching *Annie 2: A Royal London Adventure*, or the *ABC* remake of *Annie*, or *The Parent Trap*. Which version? Both! *Sabrina The Teenage Witch* was watched religiously on Friday nights in my household. When I was five or six, I discovered the perfect show on Nick at Night. A show entitled *The Facts of Life*. At one point I was some form of magical entity every Halloween. If there was a witch involved in some form of media, I had to watch or read it.

As most young children do, they play make believe based on the things that they witness. I did and continued to do so into elementary school. I have a learning disability where holding a pencil has proven to be difficult. It's pointless to try reading my handwriting so as time went on, I would draw pictures of the characters in my head. These characters would be mostly female. I have no idea why the characters of Pepper and Molly from *Annie* had such a lasting impact on my life but they did. In recent years and viewings, I often try to count their screen time and it really doesn't make a whole lot of sense as to where these characters developed from and yet you are about to read about them.

This story and these characters have lived in my head rent free for twenty-three years. It was time I kicked them out of my head and on to pieces of paper. These are some very bizarre characters I will not lie. The Magica, Spellington, Kensington, Stone, and Langston families are definitely an acquired taste. Northland Academy is not going to be the Magic School you dream of attending. There are no half-giant parental figures. There is a school secretary obsessed with daytime television that refuses to answer the phones. We have no professors that strike fear. We do have a professor that still owes child support on several children that might not even be his own centuries later. He also doesn't particularly love teaching. Our school rivals at Northland aren't meant to be shipped with our leads. In many ways early on they can be looked at as more sympathetic. If you ever have read my *Between Heaven and Hell* series then you already know there is going to be a few redheads.

In order for this novel to exist I had to trunk it a good five or six times over the years. I had to find my voice as a writer. I had to find an audience. I had to write about different characters some of which I've fallen in love with in a different but equal way to this group and some of which can stay in Kansas... Regardless, I ask you the reader to give this novel a chance. Read until the very end. Get introduced to the mythology that I've created.

Thank you and without further ado...

Are you a Good Witch or a Bad Witch?
-*Glinda the Good Witch of the North (The Wizard of Oz, 1939)*

TABLE OF CONTENTS

PART ONE

1395

"Get this devil child out of me already!" screamed Samantha. The dark-haired sixteen-year-old had always been described as poised and beautiful. At that moment, it wasn't the case. It really hadn't been the case since she had met him.

The last three days could only be described with one word; hell, as she was huffing, puffing, and screaming since early in the morning. She insisted that the birth of the creature inside her would be natural.

There was only one person left in her life, her best friend since childhood; the rest had all abandoned her or were dead. Madeline kneeled in front of the pregnant woman. She had never delivered a child. She had never even witnessed a child being born. Samantha was more than aware and was still entrusting, if not just straight out demanding, that Madeline help her. The dark-haired woman knew very well that Madeline might have been the one who was most irate with her with how this scenario ended up playing out.

"You need to try pushing. You need to try doing just about anything other than what you are doing right now," spat Madeline.

Samantha could tell that if this child was not born soon that Madeline might soon abandon her. She had every right. "Do you think I am not trying?" Samantha asked in a hurt tone.

The blonde girl looked right back at her. She wasn't going to let Samantha bully or manipulate her in this instance. "I am telling you right now, Samantha, if you do not start treating me with an ounce of respect, I will be gone. I will be the last person left from your life aside from your brother, who will pity you in the new world. The new world in which you mocked, and thought was a terrible idea."

Her friend had no idea what she was talking about. Samantha thought that her brother, Jeden had a brilliant idea with the creation of a new realm. It meant a new start away from humankind. It meant a world where religion hadn't been distorted to serve whatever mankind wanted. It would bring equality to the sexes once again as the higher power had always intended. This was her brother's idea, her brother's brilliant idea. Jeden had always been a revolutionary. Samantha always looked up to him in that sense.

Their parents never understood. They had been alright with being house servants to Madeline's family. They had been fine with being ruled by men who went by Edward and now Richard, human men who had overthrown powerful Witches. Witches had no power in a world full of ignorance.

Witches had no power in a world where the original language had died out centuries earlier, where the original scripture couldn't be read or had been replaced with new interpretations by individuals who rewrote the laws of the land to serve their own means. New versions of the original scripture would pop up every fifty years or so.

In Asia, they had their own view on things. In Greece and later Rome, humans would be fooled by Witches who abused their power. Those Witches were eventually overthrown by humankind and mankind, of course, and their own views.

This new land was supposed to be the great alternative to the new world. It was mostly left undiscovered. The residents initially ventured over from Asia before Pangea had broken up and the continents formed. The majority were Witches themselves, and the ones who were not Witches respected those that were. *He* told her this was the way to go. *He* had told her they shouldn't give up on the land that once belonged to the Witches. Witches deserved to be superior to humankind. It all made sense to Samantha. Madeline reluctantly followed along.

Then, of course, the know-it-all redhead and the promiscuous one got involved. That is where things really started to fall apart. When Samantha's first love showed up, that was the beginning of the end.

"I am leaving if you do not get this child out of you," Madeline stood up.

Samantha gave her a dirty look, "You know what? Enough of this. I can handle this by myself. You prepare the transfer spell..."

Young and angry, the dark-haired girl started to push with all her might. She was weak from battle. Her powers were still not up to par. Pushing and pushing with all her might, she started to feel the child crown.

Madeline saw as she put several herbs into a kettle. "Don't stop. Once this child is finally out of me, I want it out of our lives for good."

Finally, she delivered the child. A boy: he looked like *him*, brown hair and eyes, and a slight natural tan about him. His father would never meet the child *he* had created in *his* image.

"Well, are you ready?" Samantha barked.

"You have no desire to even spend a moment longer with your child?" Madeline asked.

Samantha could easily tell that her friend was having a change of heart. "Do not feel anything for this child Madeline."

"He is not ours. He never was ours. Now first...," she took a bottle that had been next to her the entire day. It was a binding potion. This child was never to know he was powerful. Potentially the most powerful child that would ever exist if he was trained properly.

She forced the baby to drink every last drop, whether he wanted to or not. She then handed the baby to Madeline. "I told you once, and I will tell you only once more. Dispose of the child."

Madeline nodded, "*Mitte puerum huius in futurum. Mitte puerum huius temporis ad magica, ubi est tantum fabula.*" A portal opened. It was small and red to mimic that of a child going through the womb once again. It took a few minutes, but the child was gone. Samantha stood up. She clearly was not in any shape to be doing so, and yet she couldn't give a damn. "Well, come on... We have packing and planning to do. Jeden will be expecting us soon."

CHAPTER ONE

THE NORTHLAND SCHOOL

2007

Northland was not the school that you spent the entire summer holiday missing. It was the school that you spent the entire school year waiting for Summer to start. This school was such a dump. He looked around Dean Smythe's office. The last Dean had some form of class, but this waste of a paycheck made it feel like they were in a lower-level office of the Capital Building; which rumor had it he had come from? The Capital Building... It made the teenage boy laugh a tiny bit. The only people who worked on the first level of the Capital Building were people with no drive.

Smythe gave him a dirty look. "Aaron-Richard Mitchel Langston!" he spat with fury in his eye.

The brown-haired teen stood up, towering over the short Dean Smythe, "How many times must I remind you? I do not go by my full name. The few that I bestow the honor of addressing me by my full name are not second-rate educators."

So, many Deans had come and gone over the twelve years in which the Langston child had attended Northland Academy. So, many not-so-worthy advocates.

"We know that you threw that off-campus party," Smythe explained.

Aarick chuckled and got out his phone, "I did no such thing. Might I suggest investigating Ward or Kensington? Cheap beer and loud music. Well, that's more their scene than mine." This was true. His idea of a good night was different than many of his contemporaries, which is why the Langston child often intimidated others and had many envious piers.

Aarick continued to look at his phone.

"Give me that!" the dark-skinned older gentlemen screamed at Aaron-Richard. He yanked the cellphone out of the boy's hand.

"I would suggest giving that back."

That voice did not come from Aaron-Richard. Smythe took a deep breath and turned around.

He quickly put on a very fake smile, "My queen, what brings you to your school today?" Smythe clearly was in terror of his boss.

The tall, dark-haired woman laughed. It was an intimidating laugh as it was so bleak. The way she walked, the way she spoke; there were no others like her. "Good, you remember I am your Queen and not the other way around," as she put out her hand gesturing for Aaron-Richard's phone. Smythe reluctantly gave it to her.

She looked at the teenage boy, "Here you are, Aarick."

The Langston child took the phone and took his rightful place next to the Queen. "Thank you."

Smythe looked at the two figures and was ready to bash his head into the wall. "You know this is starting to get out of hand, Magisha… I'm supposed to be in history class or potion lab, or something along those lines right now. Yet, here I am once again with this…" he looked at Smythe up and down, "Person that you hired."

Magisha looked at Smythe with the same snobbish demeanor that Aarick did. "Yes… I suppose that is true."

She gave Smythe this look as if he was supposed to know exactly how to respond. "Well, say you are sorry to the boy. He is clearly busier than you."

Aarick wanted to chuckle but didn't. It made the entire situation more comical in the long run. It was obvious that Smythe was not about to get his way. It wouldn't be the first time, and it wasn't the last time.

"I am so sorry."

The Queen rolled her eyes, "Work on your lying. You're an educator, for crying out loud."

She looked at Aarick, "Are you going to be, ok? Is there anything that I can do to make this situation less difficult for you?"

Aarick put his phone away. He held his head high and rolled his eyes back into his head practically. The teenager scoffed, "Well, I suppose you could get me out of class for the rest of the day. I'm too distraught to continue with my studies."

She nodded, "Well, of course." The queen looked at her watch, "Well, I must be going."

"Oh, wait one second! Since you are here, I thought that this might be the time to tell you…" The Dean was up to something, and Aarick knew that there was trouble brewing. Not the good kind of trouble that he enjoyed watching either.

"What on earth could you possibly want?" the Queen asked her idiot citizen.

The Dean took a deep breath. Aarick could tell that whatever was about to come out of his mouth would probably piss him off.

"Well, a new boy is starting soon. He will need a room."

The two righteous figures looked at one another. They both indicated they had no idea where this subject matter was heading. "If you don't have a room for him, then I suppose, just get rid of his offer. Did you really need me to tell you this?" Magisha asked the idiot.

"It's just... We have a room," he looked at Aarick. "He has that suite to himself."

Aarick shot him a nasty look, Yes, I have a double suite. My father pays good money for that luxury.

It always annoyed Aarick when people made him play the father card. Yet, he was forced to play it over and over again.

"It would just be for the rest of the semester," Dean Smythe explained.

Magisha shook her head. The Dean could tell this was annoying her. He was glad it was. "If Aarick wants to share, then fine. If he doesn't want to, then I'm not going to make him."

This clearly took Smythe a bit back. It shocked Aarick, but Smythe honestly thought he was going to get his way.

"Could you just maybe do it for the semester?" Smythe asked.

"No," Aarick said, "I'll speak with you soon, Magisha." He stormed out of the ill-decorated office and hid on the other side for a moment to see how this would play out.

The Queen looked at the employee, "Don't make me fire you..." A giant cloud of blue smoke formed around her, and she was gone once more.

Smythe stomped his foot. He stormed over to his desk and pounded his fist. He started to hear laughter. "Don't think I am done. We will get what we wanted!" The Dean screamed out loud.

***

The Queen's office was on the 10,000th floor of the Capital Building. It was located straight across the street from the Northland School, a property she had purchased sometime back in the 1800s to spite someone. Her office had white marble floors with dark blue walls. There was one window that covered the entire wall behind her desk. You couldn't see anything out the window as it was so far up. She usually kept the curtains mostly drawn back. A blue-toned fire over dry ice was also usually drawn. Bookshelves were scattered around the office. Her white marble desk was unnecessarily large. An even larger computer stood above it with an intercom. Magisha pressed the button, "Get in here!" She rubbed her head and then pressed it again, "As in now!"

Waddling could be heard from clear across the room with a sound of clacking that followed. In walked a plump short woman with unnaturally curly blonde hair.

"I'm in the middle of my stories!" spoke the woman with a thick New York-style accent.

Magisha ripped off her crown and let her hair down. She then unzipped her dress and walked over to one of the couches wearing nothing but a pair of black stilettos and undergarments. She plopped herself down, "Why did I agree to hire Dean Smythe?"

"He's the only one who wanted the job," Maude pointed out.

"I don't remember him being that obnoxious," the dark-haired ruler admitted.

Maude shrugged, "I don't know. You don't let me in on your weird hiring choices." She looked out into the other room where her desk and television set were. "Can I get back? The commercial is almost over!"

Was it really this difficult to have a conversation with her best friend and damn employee?

"You record every episode. Don't act like you have no way of watching." She never could understand what Maude liked about those damn soap operas. They were all the same, and they just went on and on forever.

"I really don't want to get behind. The message boards don't like it when you get behind," Maude admitted.

Magisha knew that regardless of how she felt about those stupid soap operas, Maude had built her life around them. At least her life of the last hundred or so. How long had it been since Magisha first employed Maude? They had known each other since their early childhood, but it had only been a few centuries since they had worked together. It seemed that neither woman wanted to be the one to say out loud that they probably were not meant to be boss and employee.

The Queen looked at her best friend, "Stop thinking about *All My Life to Live* or *Between Heaven and Hell* or whatever the heck those shows are called. We have bigger fish to fry right now."

"I was watching *A Model Life,* if you must know," Maude said this as if she was making a serious point as to how different all the shows were. The dark-haired ruler threw a pillow at her secretary, "Just shut up and listen to me ramble! Aarick Langston keeps finding himself in more and more trouble with this new Dean as of late. I think we are going to have to fire him."

Maude nodded. "I remember when Smythe was a student at Northland. Very obnoxious even back then. I think he was brought up in the Human Realm." This made all the sense in the world. Human

Realm Witches never fit in. They always had this sense of rules that no one else lived by. "He can go straight back to where he came from. He has been nothing but trouble for all of us." Magisha said under her breath.

Just then, the door to Magisha's office quickly pushed open, "Why on earth did my credit card stop working?" a tall brunet girl who had similar features to Magisha asked.

"Oh, for crying out loud, I thought you were off modeling in Europe or something," Magisha whined.

She stood up. The girl looked the Queen up and down, "I see we just aren't wearing clothes at all during the day anymore." She turned and looked at the secretary, "Hi, Maude!" The girl said. "Hi, Gemmy!" Maude said back. Gem Stone was the younger sister of Magisha. Magisha raised her younger sister and might have been the only child that Magisha actually ever raised. She had five or six children of her own. Magisha had their own parents deemed incapable of raising Gem for reasons unknown, as the two Stone women's parents were long thought to be missing. There was a rumor that Magisha had them killed. This was just a rumor, of course. It always made Magisha laugh.

"Are you going to give me my money or not?" Gem asked her sister. "Your money? Do you mean the money I allow you to spend from my accounts? I'm sure it was just a mix-up. You didn't need to come back to the Magic Realm," Magisha stated. She went into her drawer and pulled out a new credit card. There must have been over a hundred in there. Magisha never used any of them. As Queen of the Realm, most things were given to her. That didn't mean that she didn't have her own investments outside of ruling the Realm, Northland being one of them. It was definitely not one of her more profitable investments.

The door once again slammed open, "Why has my budget been cut in half?" demanded a well-dressed for less man. He had the most alluring well-read blue eyes and dark brown hair. This meant everything and nothing to the Queen all at once.

Magisha looked at Maude, "We really need to fire that security guard if he is going to keep letting these morons into my office." She sat down and rubbed her forehead.

Looking up, she realized that the man was still there. "Salloom, Oh, for crying out loud, I have nothing to do with your budget! Blame the incompetent Dean I hired." Magisha said annoyed.

He crossed his arms. Winston Salloom huffed and puffed, "I already did. He said that it was on you for not giving him enough money for the meal program." The reluctant teacher stated. Magisha blinked. "I'm firing that man," Magisha said under her breath. She didn't have time to deal with this. The Queen once again went into her desk drawer and pulled out another credit card. She threw it at Salloom. "Go crazy!" The three people continued to look at her. "You can all leave." Maude started to run towards the door. "Not you Maude!" Magisha called. The secretary stomped her foot on the floor, "Damn it!" she screamed.

Gem and Salloom both looked at one another and nodded. The two said nothing to either of the others in the office and walked out into the lobby. Maude's soap opera had just ended. They got on to the elevator.

"She is clearly up to something," Gem pointed out. "She is always up to something," Salloom grumbled. "I can't believe you married her five times," Gem stated. "It was seven," he grumbled.

***

"Northland School is falling down... Falling down... Northland School is falling down...," sang Sally Magica as she flipped through a book on a bench. Sally Magica was eight or nine years old. No one really bothered to figure out her exact age as she was neither the youngest nor oldest of many siblings.

The young girl had attended Northland alongside her older sister Mollie. Mollie was the head cheerleader of Northland and one of the most popular Witches at the elusive school.

The young girl grew bored of her surroundings and longed for the day that she could exit the school. She might have been young, but she had already realized that there must be more to the world than the gates of Northland. Her older sister cared about marriage and money. Sally cared about adventure. There was no adventure to be found at Northland.

"Hello, Sally," Aarick said, as he walked past her down the path. The brown-haired Magica sister jumped up from the bench and started to follow Aarick down the path, "Where are you headed?" She asked him. Aarick turned and looked at her, "Just your sister's dorm. I presume she is there?" That was a question for someone to whom Mollie actually spoke to. "Well, she could be in town shopping," Sally pointed out. He laughed, "I have it under good authority that your sister spent her entire allowance on another bag." Aarick explained.

This didn't shock Sally. Mollie had an obvious shopping addiction, especially for just about any item that happened to be pink. "It wasn't even a Birkin this time." Sally said as if this changed something. The Langston boy smirked, "Not every bag needs to be a dig at Larisa Dearest."

Larisa was the Magica sister's mother. She was a Realm-defying fashion designer. Neither Mollie nor Sally were very fond of their mother. Even at a young age, Sally knew that the Magica family was not a functioning family. It seemed like that was the case for most students at Northland. It was probably true of most boarding school students in general.

"I'm not entirely sure Mollie would agree with that. If it doesn't cost as much as a home, then why bother purchasing it?" Sally joked. The Magica sisters were not close. It was hard to tell if Aarick humored Sally because she was young or if he genuinely enjoyed her presence.

Since she was born, it had always been the Mollie, Aarick, and Pepper show with Sally in a guest-starring role as the annoying younger sister in their almost *Disney Channel-like* silly adventures.

As the thought of Pepper-Ann Spellington went into her head, the actual entity walked past them. Aarick gave a brief smile and waved, "Hello Pepper." He said ever so casually. It was hard to say if Sally was any fonder of Pepper than she was of her own sister Mollie. Ironically, Pepper and Mollie did not have much fondness for one another themselves. The red-haired Spellington with the emerald green eyes, was a sight for sore eyes, but the Spellington daughter couldn't give a damn about her looks whatsoever. Pepper was about books, not looks. She studied day and night. She had been Mollie's roommate since their first year at Northland.

Pepper flashed Aarick a quick smile, "Aarick. Sally." She then put the book she was reading down, "Aarick! You missed the end of Salloom's lecture. I recorded it, don't worry. However, that is not the point. The point..., well, you didn't hear it from me, but apparently, we are getting a new student." Pepper said eagerly. This made the boy chuckle, "I heard. Male supposedly," Aarick stated. Pepper gave a very fake smile. Sally was unsure if Aarick could tell, but she sure could. "Well, good - a new boy toy for the pink princess to fall for," Pepper said sarcastically.

Sally was unsure of what to think of Pepper. She was pleasant towards her, but Pepper seemed to pride herself on her intellect until it came to Aarick. That was when she turned into a bumbling gossip, a pale imitation of Mollie.

"So, I heard a little rumor that you three were going to the Human Realm soon." Sally said as she didn't believe the gossip to be true. Aarick gave her a little smile that practically said, *you snooping little devil.* "Weellll...," as Aarick always pronounced the word, "We just might be. Nothing fun. Just some general exploration." He said it as if it really was going to be boring.

"I said I'd take the two of you, but I swear there is nothing interesting about Humans. They are boring and predictable creatures," Pepper stated as she sat down on a bench. The bench of legend...

Aarick froze in place, *"I don't want to be here." A young Aaron-Richard stated on his phone, sitting on the same exact bench. "Nanny Flynn, pick me up. I'm supposed to be at Orion Oakland." The Langston child was all of five years old. He looked into the courtyard. The fountain was unbearably loud. The grass was far too green. It matched the green uniforms a little too well. Witches were wandering around all over the campus. It was too overwhelming for the young child. It would be something that he would deal with throughout the years to come as well. "I'm not staying," he screamed as he slammed his phone shut.*

It was then that a bottle fell into his lap. Aarick immediately jumped up. It wasn't a regular bottle that had fallen out of nowhere. It was clearly a genie bottle. The brown-haired boy looked in both directions as well as up. He then rubbed the bottle, and immediately a cloud of green smoke shot from the long tube. It was a rather threatening shade of green. "I swear, Mollie Magica! If you rub my bottle one more time!" screamed the young genie. This girl happened to be a somewhat familiar redhead. The redhead herself happened to recognize the Langston boy. "Aaron-Richard?" she said, startled. This sort of made Aarick smile, "Well... Pepper-Ann Spellington. I haven't seen you since we were three or something?" Their parents had run in the same circle. Yet, for whatever reason, they had fallen out of touch, it seemed in the last few years.

All of a sudden, a blonde girl wearing head-to-toe pink came running over, "I'm sorry! I didn't mean to drop it out the window!" She realized that Aarick was there himself. "Oh... Aaron-Richard. Long time no see!" she laughed nervously...

Aarick immediately unfroze, "Weird, I just had a full-on vision of my first day at Northland again. It's been happening more and more lately." He lamented.

Aarick had the power to see the future and the past. It was said to be one of the rarest powers in white-Magic. It was not uncommon for creatures such as seers or profits to have these powers, but they were unreliable sources that tended to live in the Demented Realm. The ability to see both an accurate portrayal of the past and a glimpse at an outcome in the future was dangerous. It meant that Aarick technically knew all that was and was to come. However, the young Witch had no idea how to use the power.

Sally smiled, "I wish I had the ability to see the future. All I get is the stupid ability to hear other's thoughts, and even then, the school made me bind that power." Which annoyed Sally to no end.

Witches were each bestowed with a gift at their birth. A special power that they brought into the universe. They were not necessarily unique. Many people could hear the thoughts of others or hover, or many other special gifts. It was not uncommon over time for a Witch to possess multiple special gifts.

"I personally never saw a reason to need to know the future. I enjoy the unpredictability of it," Pepper explained as she turned pages on the book she was reading.

She looked up briefly, "Mostly because I'm always one hundred percent correct with my prediction. Usually within a three percent room for error," she explained.

If Sally were honest, she was not the fondest of Pepper. She liked Pepper more than her own sister, but that was mostly because Mollie refused to spend time with her. Pepper would spend time with her, but it was usually done in a way that felt as if Pepper was humoring her. It seemed that aside from Aarick, Pepper was not fond of any other person. often wondered if Pepper had a crush on him. A crush that he clearly did not seem to have back, or he would have acted on it. If anything, Sally honestly saw Aarick with her own sister, Mollie.

However, Mollie was too wild to be tamed by someone who was just as chaotic as Aarick. Even at a young age, Sally could see that.

CHAPTER TWO

THINK PINK, ACT NATURAL

Mollie M Magica preferred to believe that ignorance was indeed bliss. Why waste an education on someone who was never going to use it? Yes, that was how Mollie felt about school. She intended on being a serial housewife. Her mother was a fashion designer known in the Human Realm for her department store clothing line. Her mother had no choice but to work, though. She had more children than the little old lady who lived in a shoe. Larissa Magica most definitely did not know what to do.

It wasn't an act of resentment towards her mother; it was just realizing that she could do it better than her own mother, who had been disinherited by her own parents after marrying. However, this man wasn't even Mollie nor Sally's father. No. Mollie and Sally were the results of a curse.

They technically did not have a father, nor did the majority of their siblings. Only the first eight of her brothers and sisters had fathers— the first four with her actual husband who went missing years ago.

Then, the next four, who were quadruplets, were the result of an affair with Zeus. Larissa did not know that at the time. She thought that he was just some important businessman. However, much like anyone who slept with Zeus, his actual wife Hera had her revenge; Larissa was cursed to have one hundred children over three centuries.

Larissa was only in her forties. Mollie was child number twelve. Sally was child number fifteen. The two happened to be thrown into the same school together, with the others off elsewhere.

Mollie knew that it was better to play ignorance in situations and just enjoy life. She would one day marry and be a housewife and let someone else take care of her. Until that day came, boys were play-toys, and at thirteen years old, the door to the toy store was just opening for her.

The blonde-haired, blue-eyed Magica girl walked down the street wearing head to toe pink everything. She wore four-inch stiletto heels and had a Birkin on her shoulder. If you didn't know who she was, you would assume she was an adult, which was why no one was batting an eye at the fact that a thirteen-year-old was wandering around the city of Hallowton in the middle of the day. The girl took her sunglasses off for a brief second as she saw a familiar face crossing her path.

"Gem! Is that really you?" Mollie had known Gem Stone practically since birth. Gem, unlike Mollie, was actually in her twenties. "Mollie, what on earth are you doing out of class?" the princess asked the young girl. This made Mollie scoff, "I'm just enjoying freedom!"

The princess couldn't help but laugh at this, "You will have forever to enjoy freedom. Until then, you really should be in class. You have Professor Salloom. You are in good hands," Gem explained to her. Mollie disagreed entirely. Salloom was hard on her. He made her study when she was in his presence. He made her do any number of things that she felt were useless to her actual upbringing. Who needed fractions? Who needed poetry? She definitely didn't need spell casting.

"I'm good," the blonde girl stated.

Gem shrugged at this. "I suppose it's not my responsibility to return you to campus. I just hope you will eventually change your mind. I guess I'll be seeing you soon. Love you," Gem stated as she took a pair of sunglasses out of her own designer tote bag and started to walk away herself.

It frustrated the Magica girl that Gem would question her when she herself had always been so similar. Gem had gone to Northland back when she was in school, and Mollie might have been in kindergarten at the time but remembered Gem not being in class and arguing with her instructor. It wasn't fair that as a princess, she got to live a carefree life while Mollie was expected to do better. It shouldn't have worked that way. "Do better, Mollie. You just need to apply yourself. You could be anything you wanted if you just applied yourself more..." The blonde girl mockingly said to herself.

As she continued to wander around aimlessly, Mollie made her way back to the front gate of Northland. She had no intention of slipping back in but happened to notice a boy around her age struggling to get through the gate. "Are you lost?" she asked while once again, taking off her sunglasses. This time she put them in her Birkin. "You realize you have to be a student in order to get in."

The boy turned to her. He was a darker-skinned boy, potentially Indian or Mediterranean. His dark brown eyes, and his straight hair flowing into the wind, were definitely doing it for Mollie. He smiled, "I'm actually new."

New? Mollie thought. Well, that was shocking. She normally was the first to get the latest gossip in terms of Northland. Yet here she was talking to the new student. In a way, she supposed that she still was the first to meet him.

"Well, I'm Mollie Magica. You probably knew that, though." Her mother was tabloid famous, on top of Mollie herself being the best friend of Aarick Langston, who was tabloid famous whether he liked it or not.

"Actually, I don't recognize the name. Sorry."

Something about the way he said this made her think he was lying. Mollie really didn't care, though, because even if he didn't know her, he was going to. She would make it a mission. He was cute. "Could you help me get in?" The boy asked.

It took Mollie a second to consider it. Technically speaking, this boy could be lying. However, he was carrying several forms of luggage.

"There aren't like a series of explosives in those bags or something?" She realized that was probably extremely offensive considering the boy's skin color. "The only reason I say that is because there could only be two reasons someone would have that much luggage. Either you are a new student, or you have a bunch of explosives." In her mind, the way she conveyed that most definitely covered up the accidental question, which really was accidental. "You know what?" Mollie waved her arm three times to the right and nodded to the left. The gate to Northland opened. "I have to get going." She was about to move along when he started to speak again.

"Would you actually mind helping me find my dorm?" the boy asked. This was when Mollie realized, "I don't even know your name," she explained to him. He put his hand out to shake her own, "Blake Aldridge." He had a firm grip but was gentle with her. "I mean, if you are busy, I suppose I can find the headmaster." Mollie had to laugh at this comment, "Oh, you will never find the headmaster. We haven't got one. We have a headmistress," Mollie pointed out.

"Who is she?" he asked. How on earth could Blake not know this? Even Mollie knew this, and she didn't even know who the president of the Human Realm was right now. Did the Human Realm have a lone leader like they did? Mollie had no clue. "The Queen, of course," she rolled her eyes unintentionally at this. She took a deep breath, "Well, come on... I need to get to the post office before it closes. I have several packages coming from the Human Realm today that I really wasn't supposed to order."

It was then that Mollie noticed Blake's entire outfit; tan pants with no distinguished designer attached, a plane green button-down, a batty-looking white sweater vest, and canvas shoes... "Are you a Human Realm Witch or a scholarship?" she asked in an unintentionally snobby voice. "I'm actually both," he smiled at this. Why would he smile at this? Normally Mollie would be turned off by a scholarship. Yet, a Human Realm Witch? Well, that almost felt naughty. "I suppose I'll allow myself to judge you later." Mollie stated.

As they walked down the path that led to center campus, they passed several students. Some smiled at Mollie in hopes she would acknowledge them. Some refused to look at her because they knew better for whatever reason. The faculty building was off to the right. In the middle was the actual school. Off to the left were the dorms. The right side of the dorms was where the boys slept. The left side was where the girls slept. There was a barn somewhere further out on the campus. The dining hall was also behind the school. A forest was off in a distance that was still technically on school grounds. She never went that far off. You could see some students on brooms, but it was pointless to be on a broom. There was a force shield that stopped students from getting out and strangers from getting in.

"Well, as you can see, that is where the dorms are. I'm sure whoever your roommate is will be able to help you around campus," Mollie told him. "It's someone named Aaron," Blake told her. "Never heard of an Aaron," Mollie stated back. She looked at her phone. "I've got to get going." She ran back down the path that led to the gate.

***

Blake Aldridge really had no desire to live amongst Magic Realm

Witches; his caretaker insisted that it would be for the best. The boy had gone to public school and lived amongst Humans. He saw nothing wrong with Humans as Humans lived in ignorance of the Magic that existed within the world. If you could get past that, then all was fine. The interaction that he just had with that Mollie girl, though... What was that? He couldn't lie. He found her to be hot. Not attractive, not pretty, just Hot. There was confidence in her looks. She knew she was that hot and knew that everyone around her damn well knew about it.

Blake looked at the dorms and sighed. If this was what his caretaker wanted, then so be it. He walked up the front stairs to the lobby. There were students either studying or gossiping or something in-between. If he was completely honest, it didn't seem much different than his old school. Only these kids lived here part of the year and probably had a lot more money than he would ever have known what to do with.

As he looked for an elevator or staircase or something, he spotted a dark-skinned girl looking angry at her phone, "Kirk! Call me back! We need to discuss that party before Preppy goes and reveals the part, we actually played in it." She shoved the phone back into her bag. She looked up. "Who are you?" At first, it was a dirty look. Then it was sort of an intrigued look after she had a moment to really look at him.

He once again reached out to shake the girl's hand, "I'm Blake Aldridge. I'm new here," he explained. "Interesting, we don't get a lot of new students." She looked him up and down. "You are either poor or trying to go for a look. I'm going to go with poor." This girl was blunt and to the point. He liked it. She had her hair in braids that were up in a ponytail at the moment. There was an essence of fakeness to her, though.

"Would you happen to know where dorm twelve B is?" he asked. It took a moment for the girl to think. Then she started to crack up, "Oh, how rich... I'll show you exactly where it is. Mostly because I want to see the look on his smug face." She took the lead in her six-inch heels.

Without looking back as they walked, she introduced herself. "Kenzie Kensington. However, there is no way in hell you didn't already know that."

He recognized the name sort of, "Are you a member of the Kensington family?" This made her turn around and face him, "Of course, I am!" she raised her arms in the air as if she was Eva Peron addressing the citizens of Argentina.

They went up a staircase. He was sort of shocked that they didn't take an elevator. Blake would have assumed that a school that costs as much as this one, would have one. However, when they made it to the floor they needed to be on, he spotted one down the hall.

"Did you really just walk up a flight of stairs in heels when an elevator was down the hall?" Blake asked. She scoffed at this, "People are on the elevator. Why would I want to be around other people?"

Ironically enough, the 12 B was right in front of said elevator. She looked at him for a second, and then he realized, "Oh, right, I have the key." This, of course, made her give him a look. "I would hope so," she said, very breathy.

He shuffled through his pocket and took out an electronic key. This opened to a living room with a couch and two armchairs. There was a plasma screen bolted to the wall. Books were just scattered everywhere. Several pictures of who he assumed were his roommates.

"There is only one other person who lives in this room? It's huge!" It was larger than the apartment he had lived in his entire life.

Kenzie sat down on the couch, without being invited and put her feet up. She looked at one of the books that were on a side table. The dark-skinned girl rolled her eyes, "My laundry room at home isn't even this big."

She looked over to a door on the left-hand side but then looked at a room on the right. She sort of snickered, "That's probably your room," she pointed.

Blake nodded and walked in. It was then that he realized that it probably wasn't. It clearly was being lived in. It was such a stunning room, though, and he found it hard to believe that a kid lived in it. The bedspread was blue and looked like it belonged in a hotel room. There were closets on each side of the bed. One of which was open and featured more clothes than Blake owned. Once again, more books, just scattered everywhere.

He then noticed a picture on a dresser. It featured this Aaron boy alongside a redhead and a blonde girl. A blonde girl who looked a lot like the Mollie girl he had just met. Yet, she said she didn't know anyone named Aaron. That was rather odd.

As he continued to look, almost snoop around the room, he heard the door open, "Kensington, what the hell are you doing in here?"

"Charmed as always, Preppy."

Blake assumed that this was his roommate and walked out to greet him. The boy in the doorway had medium-length brown hair with very pretty brown eyes. Blake didn't know any other way to describe them. He was wearing a Northland green blazer with shorts and ankle socks. His shoes clearly cost more than his apartment's monthly rent. This Aaron boy also happened to be looking at him up and down himself.

"Why did you bring a homeless person into my dorm? Once again going to ask, how did you get a homeless person into my dorm?"

Kenzie shrugged, "Oh, don't blame me; he is the one who had the key." This Kenzie girl clearly was not friends with Aaron.

"Hi, I'm Blake, your new roommate," he said, looking at him. "You must be Aaron." Kenzie started to laugh hysterically at this. Blake became confused, and his new roommate got right in his face and slapped him.

"How dare you break into my room and not even know my name!" he huffed and puffed! "Magisha!" he screamed.

A giant blanket of smoke automatically entered the room. As it cleared, a dark-haired woman appeared wearing all blue, alongside a plus-sized woman eating pizza. "I told you to put that down," the dark-haired woman said.

"Well, I told you I didn't want to come," the plus-sized blonde woman retorted. They both looked at his new roommate, though. "Aarick! My darling, what is wrong?"

The boy, now being called Aarick, pointed in furry at Blake, "I told you that I didn't want a roommate!"

The woman's facial expression turned from one of concern to one that couldn't even be bothered with this. "Oh, for crying out loud... Smythe!" The Magisha woman screamed out. All of a sudden, the Dean that Blake did recognize appeared. He himself looked at Blake and sighed, "Right... I forgot to call you. We had a bit of a mix-up."

Magisha now got into Smythe's face, "I swear if I wasn't too busy to look for a new dean, I would fire you right now." Smythe looked at Blake again, "I think I can squeeze you into another room."

"Do you just forget to apologize?" Aarick spat out. This kid couldn't be serious. "Um..., he hit me." Blake said quietly. He looked at Kenzie to confirm it. "Oh, he totally did." Kenzie nodded but didn't look concerned. Magisha rubbed her forehead. "Shame... Shame... It wouldn't have happened had you not broke into his room." Was this woman seriously blaming him for getting hit? "How can you say that?" Blake asked. He clearly sounded hurt.

"Smythe, did you seriously bring a Human Realm Witch into my school?" Magisha sighed.

"A Human Realm Witch? Are you sick in the head?" Aarick screamed as he looked at the Dean in horror. This was getting ridiculous.

He didn't even want to go to school here. "This is pointless. I'll just go back home." Smythe gave Blake a dirty look. Blake didn't care.

As he made his way towards the door, Mollie walked in with four giant packages, "Ok, Aarick, I need you to hide these for a few days." She put the boxes down and clearly noticed the scene she was walking into. "Oh... Aaron as in Aaron-Richard. Yeah... I definitely missed the bar on that one." She looked at Smythe, "Well, as you can clearly see, I bought more stuff. Your move now," she crossed her arms.

Magisha continued to rub her forehead, "Enough of this! Smythe, I'm docking your salary this month. Kenzie, go back to your dorm." The dark-skinned girl sulked as she walked out of the mess. "Mollie, Dear, put a brake on the checkbook, for crying out loud." She then looked at Aarick and Blake. "How about this... I will negotiate a new room assignment for you myself, but as of right now, clearly, you do have an extra room, Aarick. Just let him stay for a few days. I'll make it up to you by giving you an unlimited off-campus pass for the rest of the semester. Does that sound good?" Magisha asked. The boy who slapped Blake shrugged, "I suppose it will work for now." Aarick said in a regal but honestly rude voice.

"Is he going to say sorry for hitting me?" Blake asked the woman. "Don't accuse people of things you can't prove, child," she stated. She looked at the plus-sized woman, "Come on Maude! I'm tired of this!" She yanked the hand of the Maude woman and snapped her fingers. As Blake had already predicted, Northland was going to be a lousy school.

CHAPTER THREE

AARICK NOT ERIC DEFINITELY NOT AARON

Aarick chose to hide in his room for a few hours. He needed to clear his mind. Mollie, Pepper, Sally, Kenzie, and even Maude had texted him all inquiring about his new roommate. He chose not to respond. Instead, he chose to read. That is what he did when he needed to clear his mind. Escape to a different world for a few hours.

If he was honest, he wasn't mad at the idea of a roommate. The Aldridge boy was sort of cute. He was a Human Realm Witch, though, so he probably was straight.

It had been a while since he finally denounced Kirk Ward once and for all. He had been casually seeing a girl off campus but knew that he would never hear the end of it from Mollie and Pepper, especially Mollie. They were so picky when it came to him dating girls. When he had to go on dates with Kenzie, they would go into a rage, and other girls were always an issue. He suspected they both had weird crushes on him, even if they never wanted to actually date him. He would never date them. They were Mollie and Pepper. Yet, when he dated men, it was a different story. There would be some jealousy depending on the guy, he guessed.

Once again, he got a text from Pepper. She wanted to move up their night out in the Human Realm. Clearly, to get his mind off of current events. Aarick sighed. He responded with a yes. He went over to his closet and snapped his fingers. He was wearing a new outfit which consisted of a blue scarf wrapped around his head, a light blue vest, a black turtleneck, and some tan jeans. It was honestly rather casual for him, but he wanted to blend in with the Human crowd.

He opened his bedroom door. Blake was sitting on the couch looking at a laptop. "Don't go in my room while I'm out." He didn't want to make assumptions, but Human Realm Witches were known to be sneaky. "I swear I didn't know it was yours earlier." He got up from the couch and put on a really awkward smile, "I think we should reintroduce ourselves. I'm Blake Aldridge."

Aarick looked at his hand and didn't trust that it was clean, "And I'm still not sorry for hitting you," Aarick stated as he walked towards the front door. "I'll give you this bit of advice. Stay away from Kensington. She's completely nuts." He turned the knob and walked out, slamming the door behind him. Aarick had to admit. He did have a nice smile. If his father gave a damn about him, maybe he would try using this Blake kid as a way to piss him off. However, Aarick only saw his father once a year if that. He saw his mother even less than that. Ryder and Evangelista were not exactly family-friendly creatures.

He made his way down to the lobby, where he found Pepper and Mollie. Mollie was arguing with Sally, "No... You can't come with us." The blonde Magica told the brown haired one. He wished that Mollie would show a little more kindness to her sister. Aarick had two older sisters, and they both treated him very poorly. "Oh, really, I don't mind if she comes, Mollie," Aarick told her. Mollie gave him a look that essentially said, really. No! I don't want her coming." Mollie practically screamed. "Next time?" Aarick asked Sally. She smiled, "I guess I'll just hang out with my other friends," Sally said as she walked off." Her blonde sister laughed, "What other friends? I have to teach that girl good breeding." Mollie sighed. Pepper stood next to her. "Who will teach you first?" the redhead scoffed.

The three walked out the front door with Aarick leading. He spotted Kenzie talking with Kirk Ward. If those two were dating, he was going to go off on both of them. Aarick was going to pay them no mind though, at this time. He had other things to attend to, such as getting Blake out of his room and dealing with Dean Smythe once and for all.

As the trio walked, they ran into their teacher, Professor Salloom. "Mollie. Good to see you. I think we should have a little study session." The teacher told his student. The blonde Witch turned to her instructor and tossed her hair out of her face, "Oh... Salloom, it's after class hours and a Friday. I'll see you on Monday, though." She tried to speed up, but Salloom caught up with her. "Oh, I will? Will I?" Salloom crossed his arms. Mollie sighed, "I mean... who is to say what the weekend will bring us?" He took her arm, "I suppose we are going to study." Mollie frowned at this. "I suppose we are. Don't worry; I have no life, so we can study all night if we have to," Salloom said as he escorted his student back on campus.

Aarick took a deep breath, "We should probably reschedule. She wanted to go as much as I did." Pepper cleared her throat, "Oh, let's just go without her. We can always go another time. Plus, it will be easier to have fun without having to deal with her getting lost every ten seconds and having to go rescue her." Pepper pointed out. Aarick knew that Pepper did not get along with Mollie. He, however, chose to ignore it because he enjoyed being around both girls. So, long as they played ignorance to their own supposed hatred while around him, he saw no harm in anything.

They made their way to the front gate and managed to get out. Aarick had permission to be off-campus practically permanently now. Pepper had permission for weekends just in case she happened to want to see her father. He happened to be a Human Realm Witch. As they made their way onto the sidewalk, they ran into Maude, "Where are you two going tonight? You want to catch a movie? My treat!" Aarick knew something was up, "Maude, you already know we are going to the Human Realm. Did Magisha send you to keep us from going?" Aarick asked as he crossed his arms.

Maude frowned, "You know very well that she does not like it when you two go there." Yes, they did know this. Did they care, though? Very little. Magisha had always been a constant in the two children's lives. More so than any of their parents. However, Magisha had to realize that they were young and wanted to explore the world. The Human Realm was a different beast to the Magic Realm. There were no consequences for them here.

Aarick was the son of the wealthiest man in the Realm. The reality was that he was also the wealthiest man in the Human Realm as well. There were Langston's who resided there as well, however, the Langston family was regarded as being very secretive. They were not in the news. They did not get tabloid coverage, not in the Human Realm, but in the Magic Realm, however, they did. Aarick was a celebrity, even if he didn't consider himself one.

Magisha had been a family friend to the Langston family for centuries. She knew his great grandparents and even before that, more than likely. Maude knew them as well. Aarick always had a soft spot for Maude because she, much like him, didn't know what she wanted but continued to play the role that had been laid out for her. To some, it might have been odd for a twelve going on thirteen-year-old boy to be friends with a secretary, but Aarick personally enjoyed it. The two had some bizarre adventures themselves.

"Well, she doesn't need to worry. We are only going to be gone a little bit," Pepper explained. Maude frowned again, "Ok... I'll let you two go. Just stay out of trouble for once in your lives." She knew that wasn't going to be the case. "Oh, we shall see," Aarick explained. He cleared his throat and held out his hands, "Aperi portal in Humanum macula huius temporis." A green portal appeared from thin air, "Are you coming along Maude?" Aarick looked up at her. It took the secretary a moment to answer, "No, I have to stay and get yelled at by Magisha," she said, the latter part under her breath.

The two teens stepped through the portal. It only took a half-second to travel between the two Realms. They were standing in the exact same spot they were, but they were now standing in the land of the Human Realm. "The air smells terrible," Aarick stated. "It's smog mixed with ignorance," Pepper said as she looked out onto the mess that was Mortal America.

"It's so much like..., every summer vacation of mine; only not New York City." Pepper was from Manhattan. Hallowton was located in Michigan. "How do we go from the beautiful city of Hallowton to Warson Heights, Michigan?" Pepper sighed. Aarick knew that Manhattan was a more lucrative place to visit, but there was a thrill of being amongst *normal* people, and there was nothing normal about New York City. "Yeah... I suppose I have to admit that." Aarick said as he looked around. This was where they would hang out, at least this time.

Pepper walked down a sidewalk. Three cars passed them. She acted as if they were nothing. In Aarick's mind, they were a giant death trap, though. He would never understand why they would drive in cars when portals existed.

"It's a pretty sunset, at least," Aarick pointed out. The redhead smiled, "I agree. It is." Pepper smiled at him.

The Human Realm was the actual Realm. Witches had created the Magic Realm centuries ago using a thin layer of the earth's core.

So, they were technically still on earth, just a different part of the earth. It was hard to explain, but if all the portals were to just open at once, the earth would double in size, both figuratively and literally. The only reason Witches decided to create a separate Realm was because Humans bastardized religion and came up with about a thousand extra rules and regulations for society because they wanted power. Humans were an offspring of Witches, more than likely because the world became too crowded. However, all the original Witches either left earth millenniums ago or gave up their immortality. It was a code that Magical beings would not use Magic to time travel that far back to set things straight because it could risk changing the present. Religion existed in Magic. Whether someone chose to call certain events Magic over miracles was a personal preference and a theological study of its own. The words used within the religious text to describe Witches as evil were up to interpretation. Again, Humans came second to Witches. So, religion had already existed.

The two best friends managed to find a park that they had frequented a few times. They would go for a late dinner in a little bit. The concept of going to the Human Realm was to people watch. "I don't think I could live here full-time," Pepper admitted. Aarick looked around and again took a deep breath in with his nose, "I mean, on the surface, it isn't terrible, in the execution of how this world has played out, though. I don't blame you."

"Father always asks me every summer and break. Are you sure you don't want to stick around? You could go to a day school here or even another boarding school. I don't think he likes Magisha very much," Pepper explained. The two made their way to a bench and sat down. A lot of people didn't seem to like Magisha. She had always been pleasant, in a way that he knew his place with her. "I mean, she has her good and bad points. I really don't know why she singles me out when it comes to certain things, especially when none of the previous Deans have ever given me slack. Some of them would even try to blame me for things that no one else ever got in trouble for. The same sort of thing with Salloom, but he is just strict on everyone. At least he means well." Aarick shrugged.

Pepper shrugged herself, "I know what you mean. It's weird how Kenzie will get a pass in the eyes of Northland staff until Magisha shows up. Then it is an ordeal onto itself." Pepper pointed out and Aarick had to agree. He would never say it out loud but being the heir to the Langston family fortune was more of a burden than a victory for him. Aarick didn't even want to be in charge of Langston Enterprises one day. His father wanted that for him, but his father wanted the idea of that. It wasn't as if they ever spoke about or discussed any summer training with the company. The very bizarre thing was that he was probably going to be forced to go off to a university and get a master's before he would take over. Again, Aarick didn't want to be in charge. He really didn't know much of what he wanted.

The redhead started to giggle, "Oh my gosh! Yes, the WIFI totally picks up!" She said as she laughed. Aarick had a feeling he knew what she was looking at. Then, she shoved her phone in his face, *"Mommy, why did daddy leave home? Is he coming back?"* They were watching a scene from when Maude convinced him to become a child actor on a daytime soap opera. They had since recast his role, which was just another thing that he never got a choice in. It wasn't that he had a passion for acting as much as he would have liked a chance to play the role again. He probably wouldn't at this point. The only reason he agreed to do it in the first place was that Maude wanted spoilers from the set. His parents didn't give a damn and signed off. Magisha, on the other hand, was less than thrilled, but a majority of his stint was filmed during a summer a few years ago. "That's not funny," Aarick gave her a dirty look. "I mean, it kind of is," Pepper explained.

He was about to say something sarcastic when three kids around their age walked over. One had brown hair, brown eyes, tan skin, and was around the same height as Aarick. He wore his hair differently and had an entirely different nose. However, there was something very familiar about him. Then there were his two almost henchmen standing behind him. Another tall but lanky boy with short brown curly hair and gray eyes stood behind. He had some freckles and was honestly sort of cute. Then there was a shorter bleached blonde girl with a giant chin. There was a chance that her tan was also fake. It realistically was, considering that it was fall. However, early fall. She had her bare stomach hanging out, and it really had no right to be doing so with her figure and her age.

"Is there something we can help you with?" Aarick asked the boy that seemed to be the leader. "Yeah, we were just having trouble deciding if you were a boy or a girl?" They all started to crack up. Aarick looked at Pepper. They both nodded at each other. "I suppose I could ask the same of you. There are more subtle ways of asking if you can see me naked, though." This threw the other boy off, "Wait, what? I don't want to see you..." The Langston child put his hand in the other boy's face. "No, you are too embarrassed to ask now, aren't you? Well, you aren't my type. However, I'm sure that by the time you are eighteen, the blonde girl will have carried at least one or two of your children. She clearly wants to," he looked at Pepper. She knew it was time they move on. Aarick was not afraid that they would come after them. They wouldn't. He just left them with enough to think about for at least an hour, if not longer.

"Well, apparently, this outfit didn't blend as well as I thought." Aarick was a bit annoyed by this. "I mean, I like it," Pepper said with a frown. Oh, Pepper... Aarick thought to himself. It was ok to hurt his feelings every once in a while. If he didn't blend in, he would have preferred to have known.

***

"I can't believe you couldn't convince them to stay in the Realm for the evening," Magisha screamed from a couch in her office. She was wearing nothing but a bra and panties. She always felt warmer than she really was. It didn't help that she would have a fire going non-stop all day long. Magisha's office was on the ten-thousandth floor of a ten thousand and ten-story building. Everything above the office was her personal housing quarters. She didn't like to be away from her office for long periods of time.

Maude technically had a house right outside of town, but the last time she had stayed there, plumbing was not yet a thing. It wasn't as if Maude necessarily stayed with Magisha as much as she sat at her desk all night rewatching old soap operas over and over again. Her life essentially revolved around them. When she wasn't watching Daytime or Prime Time soap operas, she was watching telenovela's which Magisha thought were an even bigger waste of time. Maude really didn't care. The Queen had planned out her life, and the Queen had caused more harm than good on more than one occasion in terms of her personal life.

The door opened. Salloom walked in, "I just got done attempting to tutor Mollie Magica in math for two hours. When I say that I've lost brain cells, I mean it. I've lost brain cells," he explained to the two women. The Queen sighed and sat up from her couch, "Oh joy... I get to see you twice in such a short period of time. It's more than our first marriage." Salloom looked at her, "Well, that was your choice," Her ex pointed out. There was a sound of bitterness in his voice.

The secretary sighed. The last thing she really needed was the two of them going at it once again, only to have them make up, and end up at a twenty-four-hour chapel where she got to be the witness. "I need a break from teaching those children. I'm a doctor and scientist. You can't possibly expect me to waste my knowledge on teaching the children of your donor list day in and day out." Magisha laughed, "I can expect you to do whatever I want. I am, after all, the Queen and the one who got all the money in our divorces." Maude really didn't need to watch as the two of them roleplayed. "If the two of you need some privacy, I'd be glad to wait in the other room," Maude stated. The Queen looked at her, annoyed, "Will you stay where you are for five minutes? Those damn soaps aren't going anywhere."

It was going to be another night of fighting amongst the world's most unstable couple. If Maude was lucky, they'd end up in bed within the next two hours, and she could go and binge on her shows; if she were lucky, that was.

***

So far, Blake Aldridge seemed to hate Northland. He sat in the dining hall alone, trying to eat his dinner. It was bizarre. This school cost an arm and a leg, but the food seemed to be inedible. As he sat and stared at nothing, a familiar blonde girl walked over. "Oh, hi," he said with a smile. "You are sitting at my table," Mollie Magica stated as she held a bag of takeout. Of course, he was…, "Let me take a guess - your table happens to be Aaron-Richard's table as well?" He said this rather sarcastically. Mollie nodded, "Well, obviously. We seldom eat here, but Pepper and Aarick are out of the Realm for the evening, and I got stuck on campus for the night." She sat down next to him, "I suppose I can keep this between us this time. However, don't make a habit of trying to infringe on our group." Mollie explained as she took food out of the bag.

It was hard to tell if this girl was serious or not. She was very pretty, though, so he wasn't about to turn her away, nor would he himself leave. No, he definitely was not about to get up just for some airhead blonde. "Who exactly is part of this group? You, Aarick, as he seems to like to be called and that Kenzie girl?" This made Mollie start to laugh hysterically. "Kensington? Do you think that Kenzie Kensington is part of my social circle? As if… no. Aarick is president of the Northland student body. He hates the position, but he keeps getting re-elected. Pepper Spellington is my roommate, who he happens to like for some reason, so she gets to be part of this little group. Then for some reason, there is my little sister. She seems to be one of the few people that Aarick tolerates." That whole statement gave him little to no detail. "Then who on earth is Kenzie Kensington?" Blake demanded. "A nuisance to society. She is far from a liked student," Mollie tossed her hair away from her face. "She definitely seemed a bit tricky. She knew exactly what she was leading me into," the blonde girl laughed at his response. "Well, of course she did. She hates Aarick and enjoys playing tricks on him. They hate each other, really. Their parents are lifelong business friends. Well, their fathers, at least. My mother had been friends with Aarick's mother and my annoying roommate Pepper's mother. They all went to Orion Oakland together," Mollie explained.

"What is Orion Oakland?" Blake inquired as he attempted to eat some of his meal. Mollie sighed, "Oh, well, it is just a school out in Briardale, Connecticut. Technically, that is where Aarick is from, Kenzie too. I'm actually born and raised in a suburb right outside of Hallowton." This Mollie girl seemed to be both an airhead and very nice at the same time. He was unsure if this was a good or bad thing. All he knew was that she was very attractive. "So, why exactly are you talking with me if Aarick clearly doesn't like me?" Or was that part of a plan? That would make sense Blake thought. "I'm allowed to have my own opinions. Well, I think I am, I haven't asked Aarick," she said as she played with her hair.

***

As the evening continued on for Aarick and Pepper, they found themselves going to see a movie. "That was terrible," Aarick explained as they walked out from the movie theatre. Pepper shrugged, "I don't disagree. I'm not really sure what they were going for." He looked at his friend, "I don't think that I'll ever understand Human humor," he told her. "Well, humans tend to have many different forms of humor. They are divided with all the different countries and continents," Pepper explained to him.

That was something that Aarick would never understand. Why

would Humans need to feel the need to outdo one another? Though he supposed that Witches were worse. It was all about power. At least in his family and the people around him. His father was always chasing money along with women. His two older sisters were the presidents or leaders of each club and organization they were part of at their school. He grew up around Queen of the Realm as a major influence in his life. Yet, all Aarick wanted was breathing room. Room to be his own person. Who was that person? He had no idea. He was twelve, but constantly it felt like the world expected him to be born a mature thirty, which was unfair. Magisha was in her 600's, and as much as he respected and adored her, she was not particularly the most mature person he had ever met. She wasn't immature. She just wasn't the most mature.

Aarick took a deep breath as he looked at the stars. The Autumn breath felt nice on his face, "I suppose we should get going back to Northland. It's going to be a long weekend."

CHAPTER FOUR

THE PLAN PLAIN AND SIMPLE

*"**I** said smile and pose for the picture, kids!" Ryder Langston had his hands on his hips with a fake smile on his face. His third wife, Christina, was practically hanging off him.*

Aaron-Richard didn't want to take this picture. Christina was not his mommy. Laura was being mean, and Ashley was being a brat. "I don't want to do this!" he screamed. The young boy huffed and puffed and walked away from the camera. He spotted his nanny but saw that Magisha was there as well. He quickly ran over to her, "Magisha! Magisha! What are you doing here?" The Queen smiled as she saw him. Aaron-Richard loved Queen Magisha. She was always so nice to him, even when his own family was not. "Hello, Aaron-Richard. How have you been?" She had asked him. "It's my birthday!" he said, waving his hands in the air, "I'm three years old today!" He held out three fingers.

Magisha smiled at him. She pretended to be amused. She always made sure that he felt like he was the center of attention. "I know! That's why I'm here to help you celebrate!" She picked him up and put him on her lap. He started to hug her. "I saw that you didn't want to take that picture."

Aarick frowned, "Father wants a family picture! Christina is not part of my family, though!" Aaron-Richard pointed out. The Dark-Haired Queen nodded, "No, she might not be, but I'm sure she is really nice if you try and get to know her." The young boy looked at his stepmother and looked back at Magisha, "Nope. I'm not interested."

He looked around the room. This was supposed to be his birthday party, and yet it looked so adult. There had been no effort to make this party about him. The only other children that were in attendance were the Kensington siblings. He didn't like Kenzie Kensington. There was always something so off about her, and she was so bossy.

He had even seen his cake. It was so uniform. It wasn't even the flavor that he wanted.

His father stormed over, "Aaron-Richard Mitchel Langston! This is your party that I paid a lot of money for. If you can't behave around our guests, then you will sit in your room for the rest of the evening." Aaron-Richard gave him a look that stated he didn't care. Magisha brushed her hand against his head. "Oh now... Ryder. This is his day. We are entitled to be a little theatric on our birthday. Heavens only knows that I normally am." Magisha said in an overly sweet voice. His father was about to respond again when their chef walked out from the kitchen with the cake on a cart. Their staff and guests started to sing happy birthday to him. All the while, Ryder was about to start fuming. He put up his pointing finger as if he was going to use it on his son. The father backed up though and tripped on himself. This caused him to fall over and knock over the cake on top of him.

Suddenly, laughter erupted, but it wasn't from the guests. The guests had not been laughing when that happened. They had known better than to laugh at Ryder Langston. Yet, there was laughing...

Aarick woke up with a cold sweat dripping from his forehead. He quickly shot up in bed and started to breathe heavily. That was not how he had remembered things. There was no laughter. None. Not at all. Why was he having a vision about his birthday in his sleep? This was the last thing that the boy needed.

This was why he hated being a psychic. He remembered everything. He was not allowed to forget. People didn't understand that about him. They would always tell him that he held on to the past and anger. He had to forget it. He just had to. Yet, he had no option to do so. It's easy to repress a memory that you can forget. It isn't so easy when you are forced to relive it over and over again.

The young Witch looked at his clock. It was six AM. There was no use; he wasn't going to go back to bed. He knew well enough. Aarick clapped his hands, and the blinds in his room opened. He preferred natural lighting when possible. "Well... I suppose I should pick out my outfit for the day." He went to a full-length mirror and snapped his fingers. He now wore a dark blue knit shirt with tan skinny jeans. Now that was a decent weekend outfit. He then went into his closet and grabbed a sweater which he promptly tied around his neck, "Better safe than sorry."

He opened his bedroom door only to find that his new roommate was also an early riser. "Hi!" Blake said. He had an awkward smile about him that made him look as if he was trying way too hard. "I see you are an early riser," the Langston boy stated to his new roommate. He was not yet dressed for the day and was shirtless. He looked alright,

"What are you up to this morning?" Blake asked once again, not sounding all that sincere. As if he really cared what he was doing this morning. "I'm having breakfast with a friend in town," Aarick stated. He was actually going to the library for a few hours first. Blake kept the smile on his face, "That sounds fun. I'm sure you will have fun with

Mollie and that red-haired girl Pepper."

"I'm not having breakfast with either one. Mollie doesn't get up before eleven on a Saturday, and Pepper tutors Publics on Saturdays," Aarick explained to him. He then turned and looked in the mirror, admiring how good his hair looked that morning. "What exactly is a public?" Blake asked. So, many questions from this one. Aarick turned back around and put his hand on his chest, "A Public, it essentially means you, before yesterday, I suppose." It meant someone who went to public school, as opposed to a private who went to private school. It was not that difficult to grasp this. If it was, lord help him.

The new roommate got up from the couch and stretched. Aarick attempted his best not to look. "Well, I'm going to be hanging out around campus." He told Aarick. Aarick couldn't help but look at his toned body. He snapped out of it, though, "That's just... that's just sad," Aarick explained as he headed towards the door.

****

"Why would this Saturday be any different than last Saturday?" Magisha asked her secretary and best friend. They always woke up at five AM to be ready for the day's tasks, which started with a forty-five-minute shower and Magisha hand applying makeup and doing her hair. She just felt that it looked better when she did it by hand as opposed to using magic. Maude would usually be passed out on a couch or at her desk.

Saturday was when Magisha humored one hundred people by listening to their problems while she sat at her throne. It was a relic of the past, really. However, she kept up the tradition.

Maude attempted to keep herself awake as she chugged her third cup of coffee, "I just assumed that when we were up all night scrubbing the floors, that meant we got to sleep in." She threw her arms up in the air as she trailed along, "I guess not." Maude said under breath.

Magisha made her way to her throne and sat down. She snapped her fingers, and her crown made its way on her head. "Well, when you put off a task all week that you know is your responsibility, don't get upset with me," Magisha pointed out. She took a deep breath and looked at her watch. Each citizen would get a total of ten minutes to state their case. Magisha would then consider what was being said.

"I hope that today goes by quick enough. We need to look in on our little project after this." She put her right hand in the air, "Aperi ianuam!" The double doors at the other end of the room swung open. One by one, people gathered into her court. The blue decorated room with its white marble floors was now filled with citizens of the Realm. Only one hundred and a hundred alone would be heard, though.

***

It was rather unintentional, but Aarick found himself falling asleep in the library and almost overslept. However, he managed to wake up just in time to make his way into town. This was how he knew that he had a vision and not a dream. A vision was not a state of sleep. You can't sleep while you are using your powers. The young Witch would just have to prosper through the day. He walked into the coffee shop where his friend was.

"Aaron-Richard Mitchel Langston, as I live and breathe!" Gem Stone joked as she got up to hug her dear friend. Aarick and Gem, of course, had grown up together, with Magisha being her sister after all. He always thought of her as the older sister he never had, but always wanted, as opposed to his actual older sisters, who he had but never wanted. "I've told you. I go by Aarick now. It's plain and simple." He explained.

"It's much more *Aarick Langston*," Gem said. Gem understood him. She understood him in a way that even Pepper and Mollie didn't. They just had that special sort of bond where they could go months without any form of communication, and then suddenly, one would text the other, and they would spend an afternoon speaking.

"You look tired. Were you up all night talking to some new girl?" Gem pondered. Aarick waved his hand in the air, "No... not a girl." This made him blush. "Well then, a new boy?" Gem asked with intrigue. Aarick laughed. Aside from the girl he saw casually, he wasn't interested in anyone, and honestly, that girl would probably not last. "I'm not dating anyone and have no plans for a long time. I just had a very long-drawn-out vision of the past." He said with a sorrowful tone.

Gem rested her chin under her hands as she leaned in, tell me more, tell me more. You know how much I love your visions." Everyone loved his visions. He was the only one who seemed to hate them. "It was about my third birthday." It took her a second to remember, "Ah, yes! The year ole Ryder Langston fell onto your cake trying to reprimand you. The rotten bastard!" She said in a jokingly aristocratical voice. He didn't object to that sentiment, "Well, yes. However, at the end of the vision, there was laughter. There was no laughter at that party." He said. She nodded in agreement. "Oh, trust me. I remember very much. There definitely had been no laughter." Gem took a sip of her water. No, definitely no laughing. He knew that there hadn't been. "I'm not sure what happened." Aarick said confused.

Gem thought for a moment; then, she rubbed her forehead, "Aarick, I have a weird feeling that it was just some strange fluke." There was something strange about that statement, and Aarick knew it...

***

"March forward, Maude!" screamed Magisha as they entered the West Wing of the Capital Building. It involved a long narrowing staircase. It was a round brick room that had never been updated, unlike the rest of the property. The entire structure was built by hand back in the early 1400s when Jeden had been in charge. That was a long time ago. When Magisha took reign, things changed rather quickly.

Which, of course, included the adding of the color blue, her signature color to much of the building. However, when the expansion of the building started in the 1700s, the West Wing was blocked off from the general public. It was a tribute to her late brother.

Magisha turned around and waited for her lazy secretary, "Are you ready yet?" She tapped her foot and crossed her arm. It was before nine AM, and Magisha was dressed in a blue business suit with six-inch stiletto heels on. Maude was dressed in sweatpants... still. "You need to lose weight desperately." Magisha spat out. Maude waddled into the room. It was clear that a chill passed through her as she walked in because she stood a little taller. Magisha didn't seem to care. "I really hate this room." Maude admitted.

Magisha sighed. "You just don't understand the importance of the plan, do you?" Magisha said as if it were some form of cheer. "The plan that you have been plotting for over a hundred and twelve years. The plan that took you out of the realm for one hundred of them. The plan that you have been harping about since 1723! No, I have no idea what plan you could possibly be talking about," Maude explained to her friend and boss.

It was always one thing or another with her. Magisha sat down on a crate and gestured for Maude to sit next to her. They sat together in the rounded room as the Queen had the biggest smile on her face.

"Memento, solitarium!" A cloud of blue smoke formed around Maude's head. Magisha could hear some light coughing. "Hello, my dearest friend in the world." While the body that sat there was still Maude, the person who inhabited the body was no longer Maude. At least not a version of Maude that the inhibitor of the body would be proud of. "Why do I feel so heavy?" the blonde woman asked herself. She felt her body a bit. "Did I gain seventy-five pounds over night?" Maude asked.

The Queen stood up and held out her hand for her friend.

Something that she would never have done for Maude. "Now, my darling Madeline, we don't have time to discuss your obvious bad habits. Instead, let us discuss the situation at hand." Magisha told her. Madeline nodded. "Yes, only seems right. Now the Gray Stone. Is it ready?" Madeline asked. Magisha smiled. It was nice to have her dear friend back. "We are down to the fourth to last midnight. Once the clock strikes twelve this coming Tuesday, it will be ready to go." The blonde smiled. "You've waited so long for this."

Madeline walked around the room, trying to keep up with her weight. She looked directly into Magisha's eye, "Are you sure it is him? It would be a shame if it wasn't. I don't blame you if it wasn't but remember we did agree that we would only go after him if it was indeed him." The Dark-haired woman took a deep breath. Her hair was up, but she let it down. She needed to feel sixteen again. Magisha needed to feel the rage that she had felt when her child was taken from her because of the danger that his father had posed.

"My boy should be turning thirteen next year." Magisha told her. Madeline crossed her arms and looked at the ground, "Have you made any effort to go and find him?" Madeline wondered. "I, unfortunately, have to see his eyes every day," Magisha explained to her dear friend. Madeline walked over and put her hand on her shoulder, "I know what I am doing. I can't let this boy turn out anything like the one that came before him."

She then tapped her foot three times on the floor. The stone tile on the floor started to shift from the middle of the room. A hidden compartment started to open, and from it, a giant stone hovered with a glowing green light attached to it. It was the most beautiful thing that Magisha had ever created. "It's almost complete." This made Magisha's whole body tingle. Madeline attempted to touch it. She was immediately stopped by Magisha. "You can't touch it. If you touch it, you will automatically transition into the stone character that it is meant to create," Magisha explained. "Well, then I suppose we wait four more midnights," Madeline smiled.

"Reverter!" Magisha said. That was all the time she needed with Madeline. A second cloud of blue smoke formed around the blonde woman's head. This time instead of light coughing, there was loud hacking. Maude demandes to know. "What the hell did you do to me?" Magisha rolled her eyes. "Oh, language Maude!" Maude looked directly at the stone. "Oh boy..."

***

Mollie sat on the bench outside of her room. She was waiting for Aarick to finish his lunch with Gem. She was invited but knew that it was mostly out of generosity. The two friends needed to spend time just amongst themselves. Mollie also had to admit that she was a bit annoyed that Gem told her she needed to be more focused.

"Are you spending time with Aarick today?" Sally asked as she walked up to her older sister. The blonde looked down at her younger sister, "Yes. I am. I doubt that you would find it at all interesting," Sally just would not leave them be. Aarick claimed that he didn't mind Sally but Mollie thought otherwise. He was just being nice. Sally sat down next to her older sister, "Well, we can spend time together as we wait then," she pointed out.

That was not what Mollie wanted to do. That was when she spotted Blake, "Oh, Blake! Blake Aldridge! Over here!" Mollie screamed pleasantly at him. The young man smiled at Mollie specifically as he walked over. Sally gave her sister a dirty look as if she knew she shouldn't be talking with him. "Hi, Mollie." Blake smiled at her.He looked at Sally, "And who are you?" The younger Magica rolled her eyes, "Salina Loretta Magica, but you can call me Sally for short." She stood up, "I'm going to go spend time with my roommates. I'll see you later, big sis," she huffed and puffed as she walked off.

"What was that about?" Blake asked as he sat next to Mollie. Mollie shrugged, "I have absolutely no idea." She was about to continue her flirting when Kenzie Kensington popped out of nowhere, "Oh, hi Blake!

How are you doing on this fine day?" She sat down next to him on the other side. She took a glance at Mollie. "Magica…" "Kensington…" Mollie spat back. Blake turned to Kenzie. "Um, I'm fine…, thanks so much for sabotaging me." Kenzie tossed her braids back, "I have no idea what you could possibly mean. I'd never lead anyone astray." She tapped her head, and a pair of sunglasses appeared.

Mollie rolled her eyes. Sally was gone, and honestly, she had nothing to say to either of them. "I'm going for a walk." "Do you want me to come with you?" Blake asked. The blonde girl looked at him, "Why would I want that?" Mollie asked. Blake looked at his phone. He had a text, "I actually have to get going myself." Kenzie was left alone, which was typical.

***

This whole ordeal was starting to get on Blake's last nerve. Right about now, this time of the year, he would be spending time with his friends getting ready for Halloween. Apparently, in this Realm, they don't celebrate Halloween at all. It's considered prejudice or something, which he found hilarious, because they are so concerned about that, but not concerned that aside from the Witch species, he had yet to see any other species wandering around.

The boy marched into Smythe's office. He was sitting at his desk waiting for the young boy. "Well, it took you long enough. When I tell you to come, you are supposed to come," Smythe reminded him. "I got your text and walked down here as fast as I could," Blake explained as he put his hands on the back of a chair.

Smythe stood up, "Boy, you know better than that. You are a Witch, plain and simple. If someone tells you to come, you either orb or use some other way of Magical teleportation. The Magic Realm does not do Human well, and you knew that. I've been training you for years."

Blake didn't want to get into this. "I don't want to do this anymore. That Aaron-Richard boy... person..., whatever the heck they are, is too much for me. I thought it would be easy, but it isn't. He just demands so much from everyone around him. Then there are his friends. The Pepper girl is just too hard to handle. Mollie is sweet and kind one moment but a complete bitch the next. I don't even know what Kenzie Kensington is. I don't know if I want to know either. Why did you neglect to tell me that the damn Queen of the Realm was so close to him?"

His mentor sighed and walked over next to him, "First of all, take a breath. I didn't tell you about the Queen because that was something you needed to experience for yourself. As for Aaron-Richard, the Boss wants him handled. You do as the Boss says.""I'd rather not," Blake explained.

"YOU WILL DO AS I SAY, OR YOU WILL CEASE TO EXIST!" Screamed an invisible figure.

The two men looked at each other in fear. Blake would do as he was told. He wouldn't like it. He would do it, though.

CHAPTER FIVE

HISTORY LESSON

It might have been a cliché to hate Mondays, but everyone from Kirk Ward to Pepper Spellington, to Salloom himself was unhappy with the fact that they were back in class today. Salloom received an email late last night explaining that his class would be getting a special visitor, which, of course, they would be. Why would Salloom get to teach his class?

"Alright. Settle down," he said as he sat down at his desk. The doctor was already rubbing his forehead. This was going to be a long day. "Today, we have a special treat."

"Are we watching a movie?" Kenzie blurted out.

Salloom wished that was the case, "No...," he was about to finish when a cloud of blue smoke entered the room. She seriously was trying to make a grand entrance amongst a group of children.

"No! You will be getting taught by me today." She looked into the audience of students. Aarick was sitting next to Pepper in the front row. "Hello, Aarick," she smiled. Salloom would do his best to say nothing and do nothing.

"Can anyone, other than Pepper..." she smiled at the Spellington girl. She walked back and forth in her blue power suit. "Can anyone tell me the history of the Realm?" Magisha looked around the room, "None of you? Well, we are shy, I see. I suppose it is my job to teach you then."

She sat on top of Salloom's desk, which she knew he hated, "The Magic Realm was created in the very late 1300s by my older brother Jeden Stone. European Witches had heard rumors of land on the other end of the ocean. Most knew for a fact that it was there. It would take Humans another two hundred years to journey out there themselves. He made the journey all by himself. That was when he discovered it, that people were already living there, some of whom were Magic themselves. Something that most of you don't know is that we did set up land there for a brief period of time, but not on the coast as the English Human's do. It was actually around the coordinates of Hallowton itself. For you see, my brother being a Witch, chose to use his strengths in exploring further out."

Pepper raised her hand, "Magisha, didn't your brother end up with pneumonia from that journey?" The queen frowned, "Yes, he did. You see, by the time that myself, and even your much *beloved* Professor Salloom made it to the Magic Realm, his health was deteriorating. It was probably something stronger than pneumonia, and even Witches didn't have a strong understanding of illness or medicine back then. He would live long enough to see the first ten floors of the Capitol Building being constructed. He was king for three years as he silently battled his illness. As his younger sister and closest confidant, I was elected to office next and have continued to win re-election every fifty years."

Won? Or put the fear of God into the citizens; Salloom supposed that was the same exact thing. "Oh, please do go on with this glamorous lesson," Salloom rolled his eyes. She shot him a filthy look.

"Yes, well, over time, we saw different figures come and go from the Realm. There was, of course, Merlin the Wizard." Salloom remembered Merlin. He, too, had to admit that he was essentially a conman that caused far too much damage to the Realm. He had come around the 1600s with the pure intent of taking over after centuries of hiding and causing issues in the Human Realm. Salloom remembered a lone interaction with him from his youth back in England. He wanted to put a Witch back into the power of the English Monarchy. It was never going to happen. Then again, Salloom also remembered the Salem Witch Trials, caused by the woman giving the current history lesson.

"Merlin tried to create an army of Witches to go back into the Human Realm. I tried to explain to him the treaty made between Magic and Human Realm Witches, and we both agreed to leave the Human race alone. Regardless of whatever mischief they got themselves into, I was not about to have this low-life Wizard, as he liked to call himself, cause a war of the Realms. That's why his statue stands in the park here in town. Maybe one day, I will set him free. Maybe..."

While that was all true, the reality was that Merlin was one of the few people to question Magisha's authority. He had run against her in an election and there was a chance that he might have won had he not been turned into stone. Salloom wasn't going to point that out. Magisha had a way of dealing with people who pointed things out to her.

"Now, who can tell me about why we call ourselves Witches and only Witches?" Magisha looked at her students. "Aarick, give it a crack. The Langston boy took a deep breath, "Why put gender onto something that puts fear onto itself. Humans created the divide between the sexes. Witches know the true origin of life. To call us anything else is just silly in nature. A Warlock is nothing more than a name that gives power to men. A Witch is threatening enough in the way it is conveyed amongst Humans."

This made Magisha smile, "Right on the money." She looked around once again, "Do we have any questions?" Blake Aldridge immediately shot his hand in the air, "I don't understand the hatred of Humans amongst Magic Realm Witches. It seems as if you live a similar culture in which they created."

The lights started to flicker in the room. The floors started to shake. A spotlight went on to Blake. Magisha got right into his face, "Child, you are new to this Realm. Let me make one thing clear. Witches came first. Witches created everything that has ever come into existence by Humans. Humans have just developed these supposed *Smart Phone* contraptions. We have been communicating with those things for a good twenty years before, in the form of *Digi-Pads*. We came up with it. Then someone in the Human Realm finally came up with technology that might slightly match that of our own."

***

That morning was a little too intense in Aarick's mind. The fact that Magisha went right into Blake's face, though, made up for it. The Langston Witch had heard the history of the Realm so many times over the years, if not more than most, because of Magisha's connection to his family. He could tell that Salloom looked bored out of his mind. He understood the sentiment.

Aarick turned to Pepper as they exited the school building. "Do you think the lesson was just a little too much?" he asked her. "I enjoy when Magisha discusses Witch history," Pepper explained.

Of course, Pepper, who was known for being one of the smartest people in the universe, would think that. Aarick wasn't looking at this from a learning standpoint. He was looking at it from the perspective of someone who was just having an off day and wished that his best friend in the world would grasp it. "I enjoy Magisha, don't get me wrong. I just well, I don't know,"

He was about to continue rambling when Sally ran up to them. "Nina Lawrence's older brother Ethan Lawrence told her that Magisha came to speak with your class!" Sally said with a smile on her face. "Yes, she did," Aarick told her. He frowned. "Aarick, are you alright?" Sally asked him. This actually made him smile. At least the girl whose age he could never remember to save his life could sense something off. "I'm just stuck in my head a bit." He looked down at his brown dress boots. This wasn't normal. Aarick usually knew how to keep it on in public, and yet today, there was just something very *off*.

***

Aarick stood at a locker. A locker... he had never had a locker. The hallway was so ragged, looking as if the building had not been updated in twenty, maybe thirty years. He would never have touched this beige-colored locker either. It looked filthy, and yet his hands just opened the lock.

"He looked at me again!" Mollie said as she ran up to him. "Oh, he is just... Aarick I cannot concentrate at all." She ran off immediately.

A classroom door opened up that was close by to his locker. A blonde woman who looked to be drunk walked out with a younger blonde. She had green eyes and sort of looked like Pepper but was most definitely not Pepper.

"Oh, Aarick, don't expect me home tonight. I think I'm going to nail the janitor!" The older of the two blondes said. The younger one started to laugh as they both walked off.

What on earth was going on. This clearly felt like it was the future. It couldn't have been the past. Yet another person walked up to him. This boy looked vaguely familiar. It was the boy from the park the other night, "Erica Langston, what are you looking at." Aarick's body laughed. Aarick was, of course, not in control. "Aw, you think that is funny. That's the best you can do. Ha-ha. All your clothes look a decade off but are all mall brands. Thrifting is so cute, isn't it?"

***

"Why on earth did you feel the need to teach my class about the history of the realm?" Salloom asked as he got into Magisha's face. Magisha looked at her phone, "I just wanted some of your students to remember a few things before a few events take place." She stood up from his desk. What on earth did a few events take place even mean? Salloom thought for a moment.

"I've known you since I was eight years old. That was over six hundred something years ago. I know when you are up to something." Salloom crossed his arms. She looked directly at him, "Since when do you brag about knowing me so well? Just mind your business, and nothing will happen to you.""Is this about Pepper?" Salloom asked Magisha as she was about to orb out. "I have no idea what you are talking about now." Magisha said as her face turned red.

Salloom sighed, "Look, I know you were close to her mother back when she was alive. I know she passed around this time," Salloom reminded her. "It has nothing to do with Penelope-Ann." she turned her back on him. "It has to do with Aaron-Richard." Magisha spat out. With that, a cloud of blue smoke appeared, and Magisha went with it. Aaron-Richard; it took all of two seconds for him to piece things together. The door burst open. "Maude? What are you doing here?"

"I thought she was never going to leave. We need to grab Aarick and get the hell out of dodge!" the secretary screamed. "I have to be careful with what I say, otherwise, the charm she has on me will start to enact itself, and she will be alerted." He knew something like this would eventually happen. However, Salloom felt that he spoke for both him and Maude at that moment, that Magisha would eventually give up the obsession she had on that boy. It clearly had not gone away. "Meet me in the park tonight. I'll grab the Langston child. You grab the girls."

***

"Will you stop being the Queen for five minutes and be my wife!" Salloom screamed at Magisha. She couldn't believe that he was saying that. The children were in the lobby of her office with Maude. She was reading them a story while her husband berated her.

"You knew damn well what you were getting yourself into when you married me!" she screamed at him. It was hard to be mad at Winston Salloom. He had the same beautiful eyes that he had when they had been young. Magisha and her family had been servants in Maude's family's home. Maude's parents ensured that Magisha and her older brother were given the same schooling as Maude had been given, mostly because of the friendship that the two girls had.

The Witch community in the region of England where they lived, made sure that their children were given proper education. A private tutor was hired to make sure that they were taught spells, math, and history. A dancer from within the community was also brought in to teach poise to the Witches.

Elegance was a large part of the Witch heritage. Being able to use your hands properly was extremely important, and the dance styles of the time were the best way to ensure that their hand motions were proper. That was where Magisha first met Winston. She wouldn't have dreamt of talking to him, though. Maude had to make the first move. It was unbecoming of a servant girl and the child whose family was in the King's court to ever think of romance, but Magisha did not care.

"Our children want to spend time with you. Then you spend an hours-time with them and blame me for why you don't see them more often. I have nothing to do with it. I make the damn time. You're the one who hides in here all day, every day obsessing over the past," Salloom screamed at her. Obsessing? He knew damn well why she needed to obsess over these things. "If I don't worry about these things, then how will I keep our family safe? How will I keep Maude and her fiancé safe? How?" Magisha pounded her fist on her desk.

She looked out the window in her office. She could hardly see what was down below. It was so far down. That way, no one could spy on her. That was the way she wanted it. She loved having a window that was floor to ceiling and took up an entire wall. It just made it more..., more threatening—the concept of someone attempting to get this high up to spy on her. No one would spy on her. Never again.

"Do you want us to go through what we did before the Realm?" Salloom frowned. He walked over to her and put his hand on her shoulder. "I vaguely remember anything because of you," he whispered. She pushed his hand off of her shoulder. How dare he accuse her of wiping his memories as if she didn't have a good reason. Nobody should have to remember what they went through. The deceit. The lies. The death toll..., her son; her son who existed, but she wouldn't get to meet for centuries to come.

Magisha turned around, "Just leave me be. Take the children to the meadow across the street. Maude and I have business to attend to." It was obvious that Salloom wanted to say something else, but he didn't. He just stormed out. Magisha sat down at her desk. She started to rub her forehead.

A few minutes later, Maude walked in. "How upset is he this time?" "You're going to lose him," Maude explained. It wouldn't be the first time. Though this time, there were no redheads for him to fondle over. "So, be it. If it is between keeping my family and friends safe, then I will be alone for the centuries to come."

***

Magisha sat at the same desk behind the same grand window in the same office that she had sat in all those years ago. She wasn't alone. She had Maude. She had Gem when she was around. Her children had given up on her years ago. A few even lived in the Human Realm just to keep their distance. Magisha was fine with that because they were safe.

"I'm coming upon the last midnight... I won't let history repeat itself."

CHAPTER SIX

THE LAST MIDNIGHT

Maude remembered her childhood. Magisha had been a servant in her family's household with her older brother and parents. They all got along rather well. Her parents were prominent enough in the community to afford servants but not prominent enough that they would ever look down on the help, which they never did.

Magisha had a small room near the kitchen, but most nights were spent in Maude's room. She remembered their schooling and the first time they both met Salloom. Maude actually had a crush on him first. Magisha ate, slept, and breathed only for Salloom, though, and being a good friend; she helped make sure that Magisha and Salloom interacted. The schoolgirl crush she had on Salloom had long since passed. There was definitely a mutual respect but also a mutual resentment. The blonde secretary would often roll her eyes at Salloom when he would take the Queen back. She also felt a sense of jealousy when they would divorce one another, as he got to leave, at least in theory.

When Maude's husband passed away, she was left with two teenage children who resented her. She was not the favorite parent. Their father was because he got to spend the majority of the time with them, while Maude had to tend to Magisha. When he passed, Maude had to become a full-time parent to a teenage boy and girl who were not interested in a mother figure. Maude had to admit that part of the reason it had been so easy for her to stay away from her family, was that she was not as fond of her husband as she had been when they got married. He often berated her friendship with Magisha and even Salloom. He was a follower of Merlin. When Merlin was sentenced to be stone, her husband became resentful.

Long after her husband passed on and her children were grown, they demanded their cut of the inheritance that their father apparently told them they had. Their father left little to no money. Maude had to work immediately after. He wasted all their savings on the stupidity of Merlin's false claims. Maude probably could have gotten the money back once she found out about this, but she didn't know how to tell her best friend that her husband had hated her.

Then came the 1800's. What on earth possessed Magisha to buy the meadow across the street from the Capital Building? It never made sense to her. She built a giant estate where she threw a few parties. A few of them were downright orgies.

Then came 1890, and Magisha decided to change the estate into a private boarding school. There was clearly no conflict of interest in the Queen of the Realm being Headmistress to the children of influential citizens of the Realm. At least, that is what Magisha kept saying to herself over and over until she actually believed it. Headmistress Magisha..., Maude scoffed at this. Well, Magisha was and still is on paper, but she seldom was ever involved in the running of the school, which was for the best. She hardly raised her own children herself; how was she going to guide and teach generations of young Witches?

Not ten years after the school was up and running, Magisha

decided that she would be leaving the Realm in secret. She claimed she missed her parents and wanted to be near them. Magisha left the Realm a few times over the centuries for lord knows what reason. Her favorite was when she decided to live in Massachusetts during the Salem Witch trials—originally known as the Salloom Witch trials. However, much like Charleston being Charles Town originally, the name changed. Probably for the best. Maude and Salloom knew why she put herself in that situation. Salloom had prominence somewhere else, and Magisha couldn't handle it.

At first, it had been odd and daunting, spending one hundred years without her crazy-ass best friend. Maude had to come up with crazy cover stories. Then came 1930, when Irna Phillips saved Maude's sanity. That's all that needs to be said on that subject. Things were fine from then on out.

Around the '80s, Magisha started making regular visits and spending time with the Langston and Kensington families for whatever reason. Ryder and Kenneth, of course, had women come and go from their lives as teenagers. Larissa Magica and Kenneth couldn't keep their hands off of one another. Ryder definitely had a thing for Penelope-Ann, but Magisha soon introduced him to a girl named Evangelista, who was the most wishy-washy woman to ever exist. She had the most bizarre friendship with those kids. Things would come full circle in 1995. Penelope-Ann gave birth to Pepper. Evangelista gave birth to Aaron-Richard. Larissa had already given birth to Molina in 1994.

Magisha felt the need to return. The Realm was left a mess, but the Queen pampered those three children, who had never shown interest in any of her own children. The other bizarre factor was her younger sister coming to live with her. A sister that neither Salloom nor her were ever made aware of.

Maude stood up from her desk. This was the last time she would do so. She had no idea what the Gray Stone was capable of. However, she knew damn well that she wasn't going to sit around and be blamed for it like she was for everything else.

The phone started to ring, "This is the office of Magisha Stone. Please hold." She then slammed the phone down. That would be the last time she ever pretended to answer that phone. The blonde woman who no longer was a secretary in this office looked around the lobby one last time. So, many memories. So, many bad memories. More than a few good ones. She got on to the elevator. "Goodbye."

***

"Aarick, wake up!" Mollie screamed at him. "Oh, like that is really going to help," Pepper rolled her eyes. The Langston child started to gain consciousness. He sat up and realized he was in his bed. "How on earth did I get here?" He looked around. Pepper, Mollie, and Sally were there. No one else. Thank goodness. He didn't need to deal with Kenzie or Blake, for that matter.

Sally gave him a hug, "Pepper hovered you here." Aarick nodded at the red-haired girl, "Thank you. I don't know what on earth happened. I've been feeling weird all day for some reason. I had this strange dream on Friday night. Well, no, it wasn't a dream. It was a vision of the past, but it was of my past, and I don't remember it playing out that way." "Well, you do have to remember, Aarick, is that we never truly remember the past as it actually played out. Your vision was an exact replica of how it really played out," Pepper pointed out to him as she sat on the edge of his bed. That wasn't the situation, though.

"There was laughing at the end of it, but nobody was actually laughing in the vision." Mollie's eyes widened, "That's so weird. Something like that has happened to me lately. A few times, yet no one around me could hear it." "Me as well," Pepper admitted. The three of them looked at Sally. "I try not to pay attention to voices in my head, considering my power to hear people's thoughts was bound from me being able to use it." The blonde girl scoffed, "You used your power against me. It was worse than reading someone's diary." "Oh, please, there is nothing interesting in your diary." Mollie said. Pepper crossed her arms, "How would you know that?" Mollie stomped her foot on the ground. As the two girls were about to start fighting, laughter once again started to surround them in the room.

"Ok, I can't be the only person who heard that this time," Aarick stated. "Even I heard it this time," Sally confirmed, looking a bit put off. Pepper clearly was in the middle of a thought. "Well then... how interesting. It almost sounds canned as if it were on TV or something."

Aarick agreed with the sentiment. The more he thought about it, that was exactly how it sounded. It was just too loud and abrasive. "Did someone cast a fourth wall spell or something?" "Oh, I highly doubt it," Pepper said, tossing her arm in the air. There were times that he loved having Pepper and Mollie around. There were also times that he really was unsure how the three of them became such close friends over the years. Mollie and Pepper were such complete opposites, and sometimes their dislike for one another got out of hand. Sally honestly was much more of a peacemaker for the two girls than she realized.

Aarick often wondered what it would have been like to have had a male best friend. He had male friends at Northland and other places, but they were just that, someone he would have a casual conversation with. It wasn't that he wasn't grateful for his friendship with the Magica and Spellington girls. It was just something he often wondered about. What would it be like?

The door swung open. "Oh, I just had to see this!" Kenzie said as she stormed in, and took a picture on her phone of Aarick in bed. It was then she realized that he was just that..., in bed. She sighed, "I thought you would be in more distress. Kirk Ward told me he saw you pass out." Fucking Kirk Ward, Aarick thought to himself. He couldn't stand that guy.

"Kensington...," Aarick said but was cut off.

"Langston," Kenzie stated.

"Kensington," Pepper shouted.

"Spellington, Magica," Kenzie blurted, looking at both Pepper and the two Magica girls.

"Maude?" Aarick said as she saw him at his door. "What are you doing here? Did Magisha send you to check on me?"

The blonde woman looked a bit thrown off. "Actually no..., um, I was wondering if I could see Mollie and Pepper. It's getting late after all, and I thought that we could maybe have some girl time or something along those lines. I don't know, just... just come with me," Maude said, sort of out of breath.

Pepper and Mollie both looked at one another and shrugged, "Ok, well, I guess we will see you tomorrow, Aarick," Pepper said. Mollie waved goodbye. "I will see you soon Aarick," Maude said. The way she said this was a bit off-putting as if there was something that she wanted to add but didn't.

Kenzie and Sally were left in the room. Aarick didn't mind Sally being there but didn't really want Kensington around. He still felt dizzy. "Do you mind getting the hell out?" Looking directly at her. The Kensington child gave him a dirty look, "You think you are so special; let me tell you something, Aaron-Richard; you're far from it."

"Here is hoping that is true, you lunatic! Now go!" he said, pointing to the door. Sally was left there alone with him now. "Um... you are free to stay a little bit longer, Sally. I was just going to try and study a bit before I go to bed. What time is it anyway?" He looked at his watch. It was ten forty-five. "How on earth was I out for that long?" Aarick said outloud.

"It was scary. Usually, your eyes get wide, and you sort of freeze into place. This time you just passed out," Sally pointed out. It had felt different this time. There was an out-of-body experience with this vision. There was one the other day as well. He never usually felt that tired after having a vision while he was sleeping, though he seldom got them while he was asleep in the first place. There was something so off about today.

***

Blake stormed into Smythe's office, "Good lord, do you ever go home?" Smythe was sitting at his desk, looking at the computer. "I... well..." He stood up and gave Blake a nasty glance, "Why are you in my office so late?" Smythe demanded to know.

"I've made up my mind; boss be damned. I'm twelve years old. Why am I allowing myself to get involved in the matters of some hundred-something-year-old man and an invisible person?" Blake had a suitcase in his hand. "And exactly what home do you plan to go back to? The apartment has been leased to someone else. You have no other family," Smythe pointed out.

That was unfair. Smythe claiming that he was somehow family to him. If anything, he was Smythe's captive. "I can stay with friends." This made Smythe laugh, "You had no friends in the Human Realm; none that were close enough that they would let you stay with them. Go back to your dorm, little boy."

"He will do no such thing. It's time," The boss said.

The two men looked at one another in fear. "I guess... I guess we should prepare," Blake said reluctantly.

"The lazy secretary has taken the girls. The loser ex-husband plans to protect the boy himself. You will do what you have trained to do. Don't fuck up. That is all."

It was annoying that The Boss was always invisible as it was hard to tell when they were gone.

"Well, you heard The Boss," Smythe told the boy. Blake had indeed heard them.

Things were about to go from bad to worse.

***

"I appreciate you informing me of your plan, but I'm going to stay," Gem stated to Salloom. They were in an alley somewhere in town. Gem had actually been on her way back to the Human Realm.

Salloom sighed. He really wished she would have gone along with the plan, "I think you would be safer going along with us. There is a safe house in Australia that Maude and I have been supplementing for years, in case she ever really went through with any of her plans."

Gem put her hands on Salloom's, "You've been a father figure to me as for whatever reason my own wouldn't be. At the end of the day, I don't expect you or Maude to feel complicit in any of this, but I'm the Princess technically. I have a duty to stick this out, whether it ends in imprisonment or worse for me."

He knew that she was avoiding the outcome that it could have on Magisha herself. Why was she so insistent on doing this? He knew that there was more to it. He had been through so many spells, charms, and potions over the years that it was hard to understand what was going to happen.

A Gray Stone was a theory. It wasn't something that anyone could prove to actually work. This charm that Magisha created could end in the destruction of Earth on both sides of the Realm. It could end the Human race. It could end the Magic races.

"I would assume that you and her children would be left out of this mess. I just don't know, though, at this point. This is not a well woman. She has never been, at least not since we came to the Magic Realm." Salloom pointed out.

Damn it, he thought to himself. This could have all been avoided, if he had only spoken up. But he did. He tried running against her in elections and tried creating democracies. Salloom even attempted to leave the Realm and live amongst the colonists in the Human Realm, which ended with Magisha letting a bunch of idiot Humans play God amongst themselves. If *The Crucible* hadn't been such a damn good play, he probably would have been able to forget that one a little easier.

The two looked at one another. "I suppose this will be it for now." He looked at his watch. It was eleven-thirty, "I need to go and collect Aaron-Richard."

They had never said the words out loud to one another, and it didn't seem they would now, but Salloom gave her a special little nod to indicate that he loved her. She gave him a look back. They hugged one another very tightly. She had been like a daughter to him, yet another child he raised thanks to Magisha being careless.

"Goodbye. For now." He quickly ran and made a gesture with his hands, "Aperi portal!" He quickly slid in. It only took half a second. The next thing he knew, he was standing inside Aarick's bedroom. He was reading a book while Sally was on the ground looking at a magazine.

Aarick quickly shot up in bed, "Professor Salloom? What on Earth are you doing here?" The professor looked around the room, "Has Maude been around?" He asked his student. "Yes, she was weirdly here just a little bit ago. She took Mollie and Pepper with her," Aarick explained. Good. She had been here. At least things were underway.

"We have to go. Sally, you are coming too." He probably wouldn't have taken her had she not been there, but she was, and he would feel bad if anything happened to her.

The Langston child got out of bed, "I'm not sure what is going on. Let me get changed." He was still wearing his Northland uniform.

Salloom grabbed the boy's arm, "There is a change of clothes if you don't want to use Magic where we are going, for the both of you." He grabbed Sally's arm as well. He was about to call for another portal when a loud explosion sounded in the area. There was no way that people did not hear that. Salloom could hear students running around now; some were already rushing to the courtyard. It was happening earlier than expected. Not much earlier, but slightly. He thought they would have had more time.

"What's going on?" Sally demanded. It was the most demanding the young girl had ever sounded. "I will explain everything when we get there." She couldn't kill anyone. These other children would be safe. The rest of the Realm would be safe. He had to only worry about Aaron-Richard.

Outside of the window, the air started to fill with green smoke. The TV in the next room turned on. Aarick and Sally broke free of his hands and ran to see what was going on. Salloom could see from a distance outside, however, and saw Magisha fly down to the center of town on a broomstick.

"Citizens of the Magic Realm. We have lived in fear or something much weaker than us. It has been theorized that Humanity came to be because of a curse found within a stone. A Gray Stone. I've spent centuries trying to replicate this theory down to a T. Tonight, today, really, we will see if that theory comes true." Magisha screamed.

"Has she lost her mind?" Aarick asked out loud from the next room.

"You might ask yourself, why would I want to do this? Why now? You must understand, I once lived amongst the Humans. I was born in the same land that they have made a mess of. My life was ruined because of Humankind. We can work together to fix so many wrongs. There is just one missing fraction to the Gray Stone; a sacrifice. A boy... Aaron-Richard Mitchel Langston. Bring me the boy."

Salloom ran into the living room and could see that Aarick now looked to be rather pale, "Aperi portal!" he screamed at the top of his lungs. "Go in. I will be around shortly." Aarick could hardly move. Sally grabbed onto his hand and forced him to run into the portal.

***

Maude watched from the park as her best friend in the world made this speech. The speech sounded very unrehearsed. It was. She was causing a scene because of a child. "We need to find Aarick," Mollie screamed. Pepper slapped her on the shoulder, "Mollie what is wrong with you? Clearly, Magisha wants to kill Aarick." Mollie rolled her eyes, "That's not what I meant. I meant that we need to find him and help him hide."

They didn't have time for the two of them to yell at one another. Maude got in front of them. She was about to open the portal to the safe house when the Queen herself came flying over on her broomstick. "Stay back, girls." Maude made sure she was in front. "Well, I should have guessed you would turn on me yet again. You were never one to be a loyal friend," Magisha sighed. She was really trying to guilt her right now. "I'm not dealing with your nonsense today." Maude screamed.

Magisha hovered downright next to Maude. She did not get off the broom, though. "I am not spouting nonsense! Why is it that every time I have a good idea, you never listen to it? If this was Salloom, you would totally go along with it." Magisha screamed. What babble was she possibly talking about? "You need to rethink this plan," Maude told her best friend.

"Stop!" screamed a familiar male voice. Maude realized it was Salloom and looked up. He was on his own broom dashing towards them. Maude gave him a look as if to ask whether or not Aarick was safe.

Salloom nodded, "Magisha come on. We both know who you really want to take your anger out on." He jumped off the broom right in front of Magisha.

The Queen looked at her ex-husband. She just started to laugh, "I don't want you gone, you fool of a man. This is between the boy and me. Where is he?" she looked behind the two adults. "Girls, where is Aarick? He is needed in my presence." Maude turned to Pepper and Mollie. She then turned back. They don't know where he is. None of us do." Maude screamed back at her. "You are a terrible liar, Maude," Magisha started to cackle. She raised her hands in the air as if to start chanting a spell when her head started to tilt back a bit.

"You are not going to lay a hand on either of them!" Gem screamed as she held Magisha's long raven hair in her hand. Magisha gave the girl a serious look for one moment before turning around and laughing yet again. She looked at the three older Witches, "I gave the three of you the world. This is how you repay me? Well, no, not going to happen," as she looked directly at Gem. "Our last name happens to be Stone. That is not lost on me. Why should it be lost on you? Lapis!"

A jolt of blue lighting came from the sky. There were two screams. Gem tried to run but was unable to. The lighting hit her in the heart, and she instantly turned into a stone statue. "That's the quietest you have ever been," Magisha crossed her arms.

"Pepper! Wake up, Pepper!" Mollie screamed at her roommate. The red-haired girl was passed out. The jolt of lightning went straight past her but knocked her out cold. Maude and Salloom quickly ran over to her and tried their best to help her to wake up.

"What on earth have you done? Your own sister and Penelope's daughter?" Maude asked looking at her oldest friend.The Queen quickly ran over to the young girl, "Is she breathing? Please, she has to be breathing. I promised her I would never let harm come to Pepper-Ann."

Salloom held his hand out, and Magisha flew back about one hundred yards, "We need to get out of here. It won't take long for her to get back." He held onto Maude's hand as they both held on to Pepper. "Portal!" they both screamed. They all quickly shoved themselves into the portal.

***

"Aaron-Richard! I'm taking you to the Queen myself!" screamed Kenzie as she burst into his dorm room. She looked around, and he was not there. Out walked Blake from his bedroom, "He's not here," Blake said very distraughtly. Kenzie could sense something strange was going on. "What do you mean he isn't here?"

Blake sat down on the couch and looked rather pale even with his dark complexion. "He just went missing. I don't know where he is. The Queen could have him for all I know at this point." Kenzie sat down next to him. She wandered outside of campus, and strange things were already happening all around town. She tried calling her parents, but of course, no one picked up the phone.

"Well, we have to go somewhere safe. We need to hide," Kenzie told him. The boy nodded, "I agree. Do you trust me?" he asked her. She hardly knew him. Yet here they were. "I mean... no, but do I have a choice?" Blake nodded. He took her around and chanted for a portal. The two quickly ran into it.

***

Smythe sat in his office as he heard screams from outside. He was gathering up paperwork. He put them all in a leatherbound folder. On the front, the words WIA were printed on it.

"Everything seems to be in place." He said.

"You know what to do next."

Boy, did he ever...

PART TWO

1995

"It's a boy. Finally, a boy," Ryder Langston stood outside of his wife's hospital room. He was talking with Kenneth Kensington.

"Your wife should be proud to have finally given birth to a boy." The two men were joking but just hardly. Magisha walked down the hall and could hear them speaking. It took everything in her not to smack them both the moment she was close enough. However, she was here as a *friend* and also happened to be the Queen.

"Gentlemen! I've heard the good word," she stated. "Where is the child?"

Ryder put his hand on Magisha's shoulder. She really wished he hadn't done that, but she smiled, nonetheless. "Oh, he is a real beauty. They are running tests on him right now." Ryder explained. This sort of freaked Magisha out. Tests? "What kind of tests?" she asked him.

"Oh, nothing to worry about. His powers, though; he didn't seem to show any signs of anything special yet," Ryder explained. Nothing special. That was on track. No, he wouldn't have been able to express special powers just yet. No.

"I'm sure he is just trying to make things a bit grander. He'll probably start to show signs of Magic soon enough. He is a Langston, after all." He is a Langston. It took centuries, but finally, the Langston that she had been waiting for was *born*.

A nurse wheeled over a newborn baby, "Mr. Langston; your son is ready if you would like to bring him in to see your wife."

Those eyes. She had seen those eyes before. Magisha held out her hand to the baby. Young Aaron-Richard put his hand out to reach her own. It was at that moment that she knew for sure. This was the child she had been waiting for.

CHAPTER SEVEN

NO TIME LIKE THE PRESENT

2009

"*All right, can anyone other than Pepper please tell me the answer to question seven? Anyone,*" *Salloom asked.*

Aarick raised his hand, "It's All Hail the Queen."

Salloom nodded, "Correct. However, do please wait to be called upon next time."

"Never wait to be right, Salloom. It's something that you, in-particular would be smart to learn," Aarick stated.

***

"Move!" screamed Sally. Aarick blinked. That was the most random vision of the past he had ever had. At least lately. It was nice, in a way, to reminisce about his old life, as he was rather sick of this new one. "I'm moving as fast as I can," he screamed back at his friend and roommate of the last two and a half years.

When the two had been shoved inside the Portal, they had expected Salloom to be meeting them sometime after. Instead, they were left somewhere literally in outer space in a space station. It was there that Dean Smythe, of all people, met them. He explained that he had worked for an organization tracking Magisha and her crazy plan for some time. That part Aarick and Sally believed. It was the part in which he claimed that he had been looking after Aarick that neither Aarick nor Sally believed whatsoever.

"We are going to fail this simulation!" Blake explained to the two of them. He had been about a mile behind them just moments ago.

That was the other part that Aarick at least found bizarre. Blake Aldridge was a part of this organization as well. Obviously, there was a huge chunk of the story that was not being told to them. Aarick honestly was upset that he was not given any updates to what was going on back on Earth. They had no idea if Pepper and Mollie were ok, if his family was ok, or if Maude and Salloom were alive. It honestly felt as if they were not allowed to know the truth. They would wake up at a specific time that Aarick suspected was different every day. Some days it felt like he slept for hours. Others it was as if he would get twenty minutes before an alarm would go off.

The three of them shared a small room together with no windows. Aarick was carving lines into the ceiling to count the days, but again it was hard to keep track when there was no saying how many days were passing from the time they were put to bed and the time they were told to awaken. The food was worse than what they served at Northland.

The days of Aarick complaining about Northland were long gone. It wasn't that he dreamt of returning necessarily. It was that he missed the mundane existence that was Northland, and he was sick of this.

Smythe and Blake often lamented the fact that they had rescued

Sally and Aarick. Aarick did not believe that for one second. If anything, he felt as though they had been kidnapped. He wouldn't ask Sally about it, though out of fear that someone could be listening. She also seemed to enjoy the surroundings very much. With Mollie and Pepper not around, especially Mollie, she was able to be her own person. He witnessed the little girl who used to skip and hum everywhere grow up before his eyes. While she clearly was independent, it was as if the two had grown an almost sibling bond, which he was fond of in many ways.

"SIMULATION IS OVER. SALLY WINS," screamed a voice that would go off every so often.

Again, Aarick had no idea how long these simulations lasted because there were no actual clocks, and they were so far off in space that he couldn't rely on the sun to keep track of anything. At least that was what he was told. For all he knew, he was still at Northland. He never actually did see outside.

"Great job!" Blake said. He patted the Magica girl on the back. Aarick was on his last nerve with Blake. Gone was the annoying kid that seemed afraid of him. In his place was this weird soldier-like boy who was obsessed with being the best even if he seldom was.

"Can we please have lunch now?" Aarick demanded.

Sally nodded, "I agree I'm starving." She walked over to him as she took off her helmet. The three of them wore dark brown jumpsuits at all times. It drove Aarick insane. At least at Northland, he could pair his outfits together based on a color scheme.

"Let's go another round or so before we eat!" Blake explained.

That was definitely not happening. The room went back to being a blank white room with a singular door.

"If you want to continue running around in circles, that is your business. Sally and I are going to lunch." Which would probably consist of a pre-packaged sandwich that Aarick would only be able to digest half of.

Blake stormed in their way, "I said we are doing one more round!" He clearly thought of himself as being in charge. Aarick had to admit that when he first met him, he almost thought that Blake was attractive. He no longer felt that about him. He was more childlike than Sally ever had been.

***

"I think I'm one step closer than I was the last time I said that," Salloom explained to Maude.

They were both in the living room of the Australian safe house. "I think that is lovely," Maude said. She sighed and threw the crystal she had been hovering above a map for over three hours across the room.

"Nothing today; we need to find Aarick and Sally for that matter as well."

The two had been able to escape from Magisha rather easily along with Pepper's unconscious body. Unfortunately, Pepper remained unconscious and was under constant observation from the two adults.

Salloom's days mostly consisted of trying to find a cure for Gray Stone, which effected Witches as much as it did Humans. It turned Humans into these ravaging creatures with scales that would attack one another. Witches, on the other hand, would become pale-like and slowly turn to stone. Clearly, whatever Magisha created was not what she thought it would be.

The Queen, who was now a dictator of both lands, would make broadcasts once or twice a week and scream that she herself would reverse all of this once Aaron-Richard was found. They both theorized that the only reason they had been off her radar was that Magisha knew they did not have him. Maude spent days and nights looking for Aarick and Sally, mostly because it gave her something to do. She would never turn in Aarick if she did find him. She just wanted him to be safe.

"I feel like we need a break from this," Salloom took his glasses off. He had never needed glasses before. Yet, all of a sudden, he needed them. He didn't want Maude to know, but he suspected that some combination along the way of his research had infected him, and he slowly was catching Gray Stone but not at the rate it would if they were still in the Magic Realm.

Maude sat down next to him and covered her head with her arms. "Oh, sure, let's go have dinner in Melbourne. Catch a show at the Sydney Opera House," she looked up at him. "The World is in distress. There are no breaks until things are back to normal."

***

Magisha spent hours a day searching for Aarick. How on earth was he missing for this long? To top it off, Maude and Salloom had actually managed to go off the grid. Those two had tried running from her in the past, but it never worked. She always managed to find them both; though they tended to always go to the same places, the East Coast and England. Why they kept choosing the East Coast of the Human Realm was beyond her. It was not that hard to track them down.

When she wasn't dealing with that, she had to deal with different leaders of the Human Realm attempting to make deals with her. She wanted to laugh in their face immediately every time but chose against it. The American Mortals were probably the worst of the bunch. Their leaders couldn't even keep their citizens safe inside for more than twenty minutes.

She seldom left the Capital Building. The bizarre thing was the number of people who seemed to go about their everyday lives in the Magic Realm. She still had people working downstairs. Northland had been all but abandoned, but it was nice to know that there were Witches that agreed with her.

"If you let me out of this cage, I promise not to hit you again," Gem begged of her sister.

Magisha rolled her eyes, "Maybe I'll let you out in a week or so. I can't risk you trying to run. You are immune from the curse because I used our blood as an ingredient." Magisha mainly wanted to make sure that her children were all safe from it. Which, of course, would include the boy himself. "I'm just going to point out that you should probably feed Mollie more than once a week," Gem said as she sat in the corner of the cage."

Magisha had honestly forgotten about Mollie again. "I will when she stops wetting herself in my office. She knows better by now. The litter box or Maude's desk." Mollie had somehow not escaped with Salloom and Maude, as Pepper had. She ended up fainting once Magisha came back over. Crowds were forming, and the girl was going to get trampled. Magisha had no gripe with her. Well, no, not really. So, she decided to take her, but the last thing she needed was Mollie Magica screaming day and night, so she turned her into a cat. A very blonde cat.

Magisha looked down and saw Mollie rubbing up against her leg. She wasn't exactly sure why this cat was so into the idea of being around her all day. She would have assumed that she would be terrorizing her. Mollie was never known for being the smartest in the room. "I'd abandon her outside, but the two mobs would probably hurt her." Magisha explained.

Two different groups had formed from the Gray Stone; those who supported her one hundred percent and wanted Human's gone, and the group that wanted this over with and wanted back the reality that they had known. Somehow Humans managed to keep their species alive during this time, which had shocked the hell out of her—especially considering that the Americans refused to stay inside. This didn't shock her.

Instead of doing the commonsense thing, they were attempting to start wars and dig for oil. There was no oil in the Magic Realms. What were Witches going to do with so much oil? Everything about the Magic Realm was made by Witches. Eighty percent of the water was not real. It was a form of non-toxic Magic. It felt, looked, and tasted like water, but it wasn't water. At least not most of it. Magisha ventured to say that if she put Mollie back into Witch-form and let her negotiate with the idiot Humans, that they would probably be running for their lives. Heck, Maude, in all her incompetence, could even do the job.

Maude had been her best friend since childhood. Centuries had gone by. The two had, of course, argued, but they would always make sure the other was ok. Magisha had no way of doing so because Maude somehow managed to take herself off the grid. Even Salloom never could stay away for this long. Magisha would never admit it out loud, but she liked having Salloom around, even if all he ever did was bitch about their failed marriages. It was never her who asked for the divorces; it was always him. Yes, she did cheat a lot, but again it was out of boredom with her life. Salloom was a good companion. At this point, though, she never was going to admit this out loud.

The Queen sat at her desk. She threw a bunch of papers onto the floor and slammed her fists down, "Aarick Langston is not that capable of a person. He doesn't even like grass because it could have animal droppings on it. I've seen him get freaked out by Animals." Magisha rubbed her forehead.

Her sister rolled her eyes, "Aarick has always been more capable of things than you ever gave him credit for. You do realize he would be fourteen by now, right?" Gem pointed out. That was what pissed her off. Fourteen years. It had taken her fourteen years to get to this point. The issue was that she started to fall for the child early on. He was cordial and lovable. Absolutely nothing like the generations of Langston's that had come before him. His father, Ryder, was the biggest tool on the planet. His grandfather was just as horrid. The grandmother was alright, but she was subservient towards her husband, which lost many points in Magisha's book.

"The cook will be making dinner soon. Any requests?" Magisha was feeling a bit nice for once. Gem stood up, "Oh, well, a nice steak with a side of freedom would be nice." Magisha laughed, "You can have a baked potato. You are getting way too thin in there."

CHAPTER EIGHT

SECRET

Blake honestly hated when they broke for meal time. He loved getting to be in charge. It was the only time he was. When they were in their room, Aarick took charge. They were forced to sit in silence at mealtime because Aarick didn't want to talk with him. The Langston brat just couldn't grasp that they were no longer at Northland, and he was no longer Queen Bee of the school. It was no matter, though; Blake was always late for mealtime anyway, as he had to check on his own plan.

Blake never trusted Smythe and considering how distant he had been since they got to the space station, he knew that he would have to figure out his own way going forward. That is why he made sure to keep the Kensington girl safe. The boy practically skipped down the hall and quickly went into a broom closet. His powers weren't supposed to work, but he hadn't taken the binding potion. They were more concerned about stopping Aarick from having visions than anything else. Blake snapped his fingers. All closets doubled as elevators. All Witches knew this.

"Going Down," said a voice. The door opened, and he was now in an abandoned home. Well, an abandoned home with a lone inhibitor.

"Kenzie!" he screamed out. She wasn't in the bedroom. She usually stayed in the bedroom. Blake didn't hear a response and got a bit nervous. He quickly walked out of the bedroom and looked into the hall linen closet, then the bathroom; nothing in either room. The two other bedrooms were also empty. He quickly ran downstairs. There on a couch was Kenzie, with another person, a slightly older-looking woman with very curly brown hair. Kenzie turned and looked, "Oh, look, Sharrie! My boyfriend has finally returned."

"Who is this lady?" Blake said in a demanding tone. He tried not to, but this was supposed to be a place for Kenzie and Kenzie alone.

Kenzie stood up. She sort of tripped on the blanket that the two women were sharing, "This is Sharrie. She used to live a few blocks down before some neighborhood kids got bored in the middle of all that is going on. Did you know that the police in this town... what is the name of this town again?" Kenzie turned to her new friend.

"Warson Heights," Sharrie stated.

Kenzie looked back at Blake, "Oh, right. Yes, Warson Heights. Well, the police are incapable of keeping people from going insane. So, when I was going on a walk and saw Sharrie just sitting on the street, I invited her to stay with me."

Kenzie was supposed to be staying inside. Blake honestly was a bit furious. Yet, if he was going to stick with his plan, then he couldn't say anything to her.

"Well, then, Sharrie, why don't you tell me a bit about yourself." He sat down on one of the armchairs. This was going to be a long visit.

***

"I have no idea where he went off to this time," Aarick said as he slammed his tray down at the table in the cafeteria.

Sally sat across from him, "We have to get out of here. I need to make sure my family is all right."

Aarick agreed. It was time they escaped. He was ready to escape after day three of this, "I should just turn myself in to Magisha. It would be over for you," Aarick told her.

Sally's eyes opened wide, "Absolutely not! You will not let yourself be a sacrifice to whatever weirdness Magisha has up her sleeves. Aarick, I don't blame you for this in the slightest."

Sally often told him that. Aarick still felt that this was his fault. Had he been too vain before? Was he too much of a bitch? Probably both. It was hard not to be. The people around him expected more out of him than he expected out of himself. There was never room for him not to be off.

"How on earth do we get out of here? How do we stop her? I'm not trained to stop the Queen of the Realm. I'm not trained to do anything."

It was hard to say what was being accomplished here at the WIA. He had no idea what the WIA even stood for. All he knew was it seemed to be an anti-Magisha organization that knew that she had been after Aarick for years. The question was, what did the Gray Stone possibly have to do with Aarick? Aarick really was indifferent towards Human lives. He wasn't one to place himself into politics in that way.

There were parts of his family who lived in the Human Realm. They were not as close with those parts of the family. His father, Ryder, inherited the main branch of the family business from his grandparents, leaving his aunt and uncle with crumbs, as they called it. His uncle married a southern belle where his cousin Avery came from. Then his aunt married an English Aristocrat from whom his cousin Anders came from. The three looked nearly identical, minus some height difference and hair color. Avery was a blonde and Anders a redhead. One also happened to have a strong Southern dialect and the other a very strong English dialect.

The Langston's were rather dysfunctional. It was not a family who said, I love you. He had never once told his two older sisters any such thing. He was not even sure that his parents had ever told him that they loved him or his two siblings.

The family's live-in nanny, Nanny Flynn, was a real monster of a woman. She got paid to be the person who would deal with any sort of school functions for the three Langston children. If for whatever reason, the school called for his parents, they would just send the nanny. It wasn't possible to get ahold of either Ryder or Evangelista. No one really knew where Evangelista even was. Ryder just refused to pick up the phone. His birthdays each year doubled as business parties or some sort of function. He hadn't had a birthday in what felt like forever. That might have been a good thing.

Aarick looked at Sally, "You know, I feel as though the two of us have created a rather sibling-like bond over the past few years. I just wanted you to know."

It was obvious Sally knew that he was unable to say the words himself. "I love you too," she smiled. "Now, let's figure out our escape plan," she added.

***

She had been sitting in this room for what felt like forever but also only a minute. It was honestly one of the most beautiful white rooms she had ever been in, and she felt amazing the entire time. Pepper was not sure where she was, but she didn't actually mind. The last thing she remembered was Magisha in the park, but she was having trouble putting two and two together.

Pepper's life had always been full of mystery. There was a longing for whether her father David was ok. She had not seen him since the beginning of last summer. He was the chief of staff at a prestigious Human Realm hospital in New York City. That was one of the reasons that Pepper wanted to be a doctor. However, she wanted to be a lawyer first. Then finally, an entrepreneur. It might have made more sense to go to school for the latter first and then get into one of the others, but she would have a millennium of time to do it all. It wasn't as if she was worried.

"You have a visitor Miss Spellington," the most angelic voice stated out of nowhere. She hadn't heard anyone in the time that she had been there.

A door opened. Pepper was unsure of who it might be but felt a rush of excitement over who it could be. Could it be Aarick? No. He was probably busy. It could be Salloom. She did miss her studies so much; probably not, though. That was just wishful thinking. She knew it wouldn't possibly be her father.

Her jaw dropped as a very vaguely familiar figure walked in, another redhead. However, slightly taller, and definitely in her late twenties. She had red eyes just like Pepper had remembered. That was a sign of the genie in her.

The young Spellington girl jumped up from the armchair that she was sitting in and rushed over. "Mother! Oh, mother, how are you here? Where is here?" She started to put things together.

It all started to come together. The white room in which she felt no pain. The loss of memory and the fact that she only seemed to remember the good and not the bad.

"Mother, am I dead?"

Penelope-Ann Ashford Spellington had died when Pepper was

three years old. She originally came from the Magic Realm but met David Spellington on a trip to New York City with the Queen herself, Magisha. They fell madly in love and married soon after. It wouldn't have been long from there that they had Pepper.

"Hello, my beautiful daughter."

Pepper started to hug her mother, "I'm so happy, yet, I feel like I should be scared and sad, but I don't feel those emotions. What on earth is going on?"

The mother took her daughter's hand and gestured for them to go and sit on a couch that magically appeared in place of the armchair. "Do not worry. You are not dead. This is not that place. This is a place along the way that people go as fates higher than we can imagine decide what happens next. I have been told though, that this is only a visit for you."

Her mother spoke as elegantly as ever. Pepper remembered her having the most beautiful singing voice. She wanted her mother to sing, but there were so many questions she wanted to ask.

"I don't know how I got here," Pepper explained.

"Well, it is all because of Magisha. She promised me that I would get to visit you one day. She had a vision right before I died that this would happen. I've anxiously been awaiting since then."

There was a lot to unpack in just what she had said. Magisha had promised that they would meet again. That made no sense.

"Magisha doesn't have visions," Pepper pointed out to her mother.

Penelope brushed some hair out of her face, "Magisha doesn't have them regularly anymore. However, once in a blue moon, they do occur. I didn't realize, though, that the reason that I'd be seeing you again would be because of her," Penelope explained. Her smile turned to a frown, "I should never have trusted that woman. The regret I have after what she did to my daughters."

This made Pepper's eyes widen. Daughters? "You said that in plural? I have a sister?"

Penelope sighed, "Oh, I have so much to tell you and not very much time. They made you wait for so long because this information had to be shared now and not then as we had to wait for time to catch up on earth. Long story short, you do have a sister, a twin sister that was born three years after you. It was Magisha's suggestion. It was your grandmother's fault."

All of this was just too much to handle. Her mother spoke in such a poetic way that it was starting to frustrate her. "Does dad know about this sister of mine?"

Her mother continued to frown, "No. It wasn't safe for anyone but her and I to know. I don't know an easy way to say this, but Pepper," the mother put her hands on her daughter's, "Your grandmother hated the idea of your father marrying someone with genie blood in them. On top of the fact that I came from the Magic Realm, it was just unacceptable. Obviously, mother Spellington...," her voice started to tremble, "Mother Spellington came from the hierarchy of Human Realm Witches. All she ever did was brag about how that damn house was the most prestigious in all New York. That house was a gaudy tourist attraction. I mean, really - The Statue of Liberty." The house that the Spellington's lived in was the Statue of Liberty. The Humans thought it was a gift to them. In reality, it was just a way for the Spellington family to take possession of the island without paying American Mortal taxes.

"Your father refused to listen to reason when it came to that woman," Penelope looked rather irate.

Pepper honestly had no real relationship with her grandmother. She never came around when Pepper was around. Whenever she attempted to call her father, he said that she was either there or around if he actually picked up the phone. Yet, she never spoke with Pepper.

Pepper honestly had given up on the idea of a relationship with the

Spellington family years ago, which almost entirely included her own father, with whom she did adore but from a distance. She stayed with the Ashford family in the Magic Realm during most holiday breaks.

"Ok, so please explain this sister of mine. Where is she?" Pepper demanded.

***

"This is the most movement I've seen from Pepper in a long time," Maude said as she sat down next to Salloom. Maude had just finished cleaning up after Pepper. This day was never-ending, it seemed.

There was a short glimpse of hope that they had found Aarick, but it turned out to be a false positive.

"Do you think we should attempt to get in contact with the Langston family again? Maybe they have been hiding him and just don't want anyone knowing where he is," Salloom suggested.

Maude looked at him as if he should have known better than to say what he just said, which he should have. "The Langston's would feed their youngest child to wolves if it meant saving their own hides, which if I remember correctly, they have done several times over," Maude stated.

Maude had never been fond of the Langston family, but Magisha constantly made her spend time with them over the centuries. Aarick was the only one she really liked. She still had nightmares of Ryder and Evangelista's wedding. They were both cheating on one another before, during, and after the ceremony. How they accomplished that is better off left to the imagination.

"This is a crazy thought, but what about the Demented Realm?" Maude suggested. Salloom thought for a moment, "How would Aarick have gotten there, though?" That was something she really hadn't thought about. It was just another theory. "It's just a thought. I could use my connections."

The Demented Realm was where the undesirable species went after the two primary Realms were created. Essentially it was where Vampires, Pixies, Goblins, and Sirens went along with whatever other Demon-like creatures were not welcome in either of the top-tier Realms. Merfolk blocked access to Atlantis from the Sirens centuries ago. Mermaids just wanted to be left alone in general, such a vain species. Fairies were just as tricky as Pixies, but Fairy kind had been able to strike deals with both Magisha and the Council of Three of the Human Realm, leaving Pixies without a place to stand or float, for that matter. Vampires were definitely not welcome amongst Humans because of their blood. They would have been welcome in the Magic Realm, but the sunlight, even though it was dimmer, was too much. It also went against the Witch customs for a species to attack Humans, at least until a few years ago, so they were banished. Magisha honestly just didn't like Goblins. They had been neighbors with one back when they were children, and she still harbored a grudge, which was typical of Magisha.

"Well, I'm going to make some calls," Maude explained. Salloom took her hand before she could get up, "I'm just going to point this out, but you do realize that some of those contacts could also be in contact with Magisha."

Maude hadn't thought of that, but he was right. They probably were. "We have to figure out something."

As they sat puzzled about where to go next, they both heard a voice from across the room, *"No... No. That can't be true,"* Pepper was finally speaking.

***

"I just got off the phone with the President of the United States," Magisha said as she walked out from the West Wing.

Gem looked at her with a little intrigue, "And?" Gem asked.

Magisha sat down on her couch, "Well, of course, they are of no help. The idiot is more concerned about negotiating for oil. I don't know how many times I have to tell that moron that I have no oil," she sighed.

"Well, why don't you just use Magic and give the damn mortals some form of oil substance?" Gem looked off into space for a moment, "Why am I helping you negotiate forms of terrorism?"

Magisha started to laugh, "You really are a Stone."

Gem couldn't possibly imagine that her parents or their brother were anything like Magisha. She had only ever been around her parents a few times and honestly wouldn't know how to go about looking for them even if she tried. She had assumed they were in England but could never find them when she often visited. Gem attempted searching Australia, Canada, and South Africa out of the assumption that maybe they had moved to one of those countries. There were no Witches with the last name Stone anywhere. Yet, Magisha insisted that they were alive, just idiots, which was why she didn't let her live with them.

"I'm going to have lunch with my head of the military," Magisha waved her hand, and a blue jacket appeared on her.

Gem stormed over to the corner of the cage, "Since when does the Magic Realm have a head of military?"

Magisha clearly thought about it for a second, "Since about three weeks ago. It's not just the US that is after this fictitious oil. On top that, they have the nerve to think that they could just stop me with guns," she rolled her eyes and sighed. "Honestly, well, I'll bring you back some food. Eat the entire roll this time. Seriously, it was Maude who needed to lose weight, not you," she walked out.

Mollie, in cat form, walked over. The cat clearly was waiting for something. "Ok, she is in the elevator," Mollie said.

"Thank God, I don't know how much longer I can handle this. She spends the entire evening rambling about things that happened three hundred and fifty years ago."

Gem had always appreciated Maude, but if she ever saw her again, she was getting her a giant gift basket. If she ever saw her again... Gem has been so wrapped up in being trapped herself that she hadn't thought about the others, Maude, Salloom, Pepper, Aarick, and even Sally. Were they ok? She was honestly shocked that Aarick had been able to stay away for so long.

"You need to try harder at getting your magic to work outside of that cage. I can't be a cat for much longer!" Mollie screamed at her.

Gem had honestly been trying to think of just about anything. However, if she were honest, while she wanted to help Mollie go back to Witch form, she was more concerned with getting them both out of the office.

The Princess looked around the room. This was such a warm but cold feeling place. The dark tones would make you feel warm, but the shots of blue and white everywhere just completely made you feel like putting a scarf and sweater on. If Gem ever had her way, she would burn the place down. It might have been her brother's legacy, but she had never met that man. He died centuries before her own birth.

Growing up as Princess Gemma Stone was a nightmare and a half. At first, she was enrolled at Northland and was a pupil in Salloom's class. That soon changed as the children in the class would not interact with her. They tried placing her at Orion Oakland and West Lake, but neither of those were any better. The problem was the fact that she was treated as a royal figure.

Gem had to demand and beg to be allowed to study in the Human Realm. Magisha tried to compromise having her study with a private tutor. Salloom and Maude both objected to this and made sure that she got her way. Gem predicted that was partly because they both thought

Magisha would make one or the other be that tutor. Gem blamed neither of them for not wanting to take on that task. They were already both responsible for Magisha and her crazy schemes.

If Gem honestly thought about it, this was why she always felt such a strong connection to Aarick. They had been through similar upbringings. No, Aarick was not a prince or true royalty. However, the Langston name was the most powerful in the Realm right under the Stone name, which was seldom used, so there was an argument that the Langston name held the highest stature.

Gem chose to embrace the status of airhead princess, which the press liked to play on her. Aarick just wanted to hide in the background and live his own life as he was now a teenager, which she realized now. Fourteen-years-old; that poor boy was going through his early teens either in capture or hiding. Gem couldn't even imagine what that must have been like.

***

"We are going to get caught," Aarick explained to Sally. Sally looked at Aarick in confusion. She never thought that he would be afraid of getting caught. It used to be a thrill for him. Aarick looked at her, "I'm just tired of the consequences around here."

Sally had never been forced into the consequences in the same way Aarick had. There were extended periods of time when Aarick was missing. He wouldn't speak for hours or maybe even days after these consequences would happen.

"Well, I know that I've seen Blake run into this damn closet before." Sally had taken to swearing like a sailor, and honestly, she liked it.

The two hid behind the wall of an adjacent hallway. It didn't take long as Blake emerged from it only a few minutes later. He seemed to be rather pissed off. He stormed down the hall. Sally gestured for

Aarick to follow her. He did but very reluctantly.

"Sally, we are in a janitor's closet," Aarick said, a bit confused. She sighed. He was right. "Wait..." Aarick said. There was a spark in him that she had not felt in a very long time. "All closets double as elevators. Every Witch knows that," Aarick pointed out. Sally started to smile, "How would Blake be accessing the elevator, though? He doesn't have his powers." Unless... the two looked at each other, "That little brat! How does he have his powers?" Aarick screamed.

Sally quickly put her hand on his mouth, "Quiet, or we will get caught." So, Blake was escaping off this space station or whatever the heck it was supposed to be. Sally honestly felt like a space station was the most convoluted excuse for where they were. Yet here they were supposedly wandering around in a space station.

"Aarick, you need to try and unbind your powers." Sally insisted. Aarick looked at her. "Sally, they have been giving us potions to bind our powers." He reminded her. It was just so upsetting to watch this version of Aarick. He used to be such a powerful person, even if his power was far from a flashy one.

"I've seen you strut the streets in a six-inch heal because someone you didn't like was eyeing them. I've watched as you've started rumors about Kensington that tore her to shreds. You've slapped two of the Deans. It's time to make it a third with Smythe, by the way. It's time to be Aarick Mitchel Langston. The one and only." Sally said with passion in her voice.

Aarick's eyes widened. He smiled at her, "You're right... but seriously, we are going to get caught. We need to get going back," Aarick explained. Sally sighed. She needed to figure out a way to unbind their powers. It was the only way out of this.

CHAPTER NINE

TWINCIDENTALLY

"**Y**our grandmother was poisoning me throughout my entire pregnancy. She didn't want your father to have children with me. It weakened me," Penelope explained to her daughter. Pepper was just in complete shock. She was in a coma and just discovered this now after several years. She was having a conversation with her own mother. Her grandmother was apparently some Upper East Side psychopath.

"So, this is why dad is never around? He doesn't want grandmother to harm me?" Pepper asked.

Penelope looked at her, a bit distraught over the question. She put her hand on Pepper's shoulder, "Your father has no idea of any of this. We fell in love almost at first sight and were married six months later. It was an act of rebellion on his end but almost immediately after, he started freaking out. He loved me very much, but his mother's approval still meant too much to him."

This talk just filled in so many puzzle pieces that were missing. It was wild to have a full conversation.

"We moved out to Connecticut for a while. Then when I got sick, he was insistent that we be around family. Yet apparently, my family in the Magic Realm was out of the question. I only really started to develop my symptoms after giving birth to you," Penelope explained.

Pepper was still trying to piece together things from this, "So, then I'm confused. I have a younger sister, but she is somehow my twin?"

Penelope cleared her throat, "You were clearly the stronger of the two. You inherited my genie lineage, which Magisha and I thought must have given you extra protection. However, your sister did not and was the one to take most of the potion's effects. Magisha was able to incubate her in a frozen state as the potion was drained from her. She was a baby, though, so it took several years. It had to be done in a frozen state, so she was frozen in time."

Pepper didn't really understand everything being told to her, which was a first because she was normally the one explaining everything to people around her. "Is she identical?" Pepper asked. Her mother sighed, "She was when she was born, but the effects of being in that state moved her genetics all over the place."

Her grandmother was a sick woman. That was now very obvious. "Well, what on earth happened to this sister?" Pepper needed to know. She needed to find her sister if and when she ever got out of this coma.

Penelope looked down, "Magisha had her adopted to a family out in Grosse Pointe, Michigan." Pepper immediately looked at her mother, "Isn't that the setting of that soap opera?" Her mother laughed, "Take a wild guess at who suggested the location to Magisha."

***

Maude and Salloom ducked as Pepper's telepathy was running

ramped from inside her coma. Something was clearly going on within her subconscious, and there was nothing anyone could do about it.

"Why can't we just bind her powers?" Maude screamed over the TV volume that kept going up and down. Salloom did a quick jump out of the way as a group of knives made their way in his direction. "It's not advisable. Let's just get through this, and hopefully, it means she is on her way to waking up!" Salloom said as he dodged a book being thrown in his direction.

All of a sudden, everything stopped. They looked at each other and got up. "Ok, she is clearly calm for now." Things were definitely taking a turn for the insane. Salloom was ready to just throw in the towel and let Magisha throw him in jail. He didn't want to tell Maude that, however, as she was on a mission. These kids clearly meant something to her. He understood. They were good kids. Even if Mollie never showed up for a day of class in her life, he knew she was a good kid. They were just misguided.

"How about we go outside for a while..., just in case." Maude suggested. The two took one last look at Pepper as they ran for the door. They were out in the middle of nowhere.

It was twenty miles to go into town, and they seldom ever did. While Australia was able to keep things under wraps a lot better than the United States, they still had ramped cases of Gray Stone. Once you were diagnosed and Human, you slowly turned into this swamp-like creature. It was not exactly something that could be controlled. It wasn't a reversal of Humanity; it was a second wave evolution with a variant that made it lethal, which didn't shock Salloom. Magisha never thought of things on a small scale, only the grand scale.

It was weird. If they weren't in hiding with a teenage girl in a coma in their living room, searching for a teenage boy, with the threat of being caught by his ex and her best friend, this would be a nice night of looking up watching the stars.

"One day, things will go back to normal, right?" he asked as he sat down on a bench. Maude sighed, "When were things ever normal? When we were what twelve?" That was an understatement. "She was normal at one point, right?" he asked. He fell in love with a person, right? Not the nihilistic megalomaniac. That wasn't the version of her that he liked. Maybe that was the version that he would continue returning to. However, it wasn't the version he first fell in love with. He fell in love with the girl who came from a little bit less than the people around her. That didn't make her a bad person, even if that was the fashioned view of things back then. Magisha was just misguided. She always was and probably always would be.

How did this story end, though? Did Magisha capture Aarick and do her worst? Did she destroy the Human in the process? Or did she fail? If she did fail, was that a bad thing? Salloom knew it was a good thing. She, unfortunately, needed to fail. He just hoped that it wouldn't be fatal on to her.

Maude turned to him, "She was normal. I think..., I don't remember. She was always just Magisha." Something in the way Maude said it clearly made them both doubt that she was ever just Magisha. Salloom turned to her, "How many potions and charms do you think she's put us on over the years?" He asked.

The blonde rubbed her forehead, "At this point, I just question how I could believe that it was normal for her to put me on a vitamin regimen for fifty years that changed every other day." This made Salloom a little bit happy. He thought he had been the only one on those strange vitamins.

***

"How much longer are you going to keep those children here?"

Smythe sighed, "We can't just throw them to the wolves. We need to make sure that they are trained properly," as he slammed shut a cabinet in his office at the WIA.

This entire situation was clearly over his head. He knew it, and so did The Boss. Neither had said it out loud as of yet, but it was coming, and Smythe was nerve-wracked about it.

"Why on earth did you let that Aldridge boy tag along? I realize he was part of the Northland plan, but he is useless to me now."

It annoyed Smythe that The Boss didn't want to keep Blake aground. It was The Boss who was insistent that he spend years being the little brat's guardian or adoptive parent or whatever the heck he was to him. He never had a desire to have children. Yet for the last fourteen years of his life, he spent it with a child.

"I didn't feel comfortable just letting him get stuck in the mess down there," which he knew wasn't going to matter to The Boss. They never cared about how people felt, only how it would affect what they wanted.

"I want him removed once and for all. Blake seems to think that he is in charge. Aaron-Richard is in charge; at least he must think he is in charge. I'm also disappointed that you brought me the wrong Magica girl."

It was as if he could never do anything right. "All you told me was that it wasn't Mollie. I just assumed you meant Sally. There are how many Magica girls? Larissa is still popping out babies even during this nonsense." Smythe was not above pointing out the obvious.

"Oh, calm down! Salina works too. She is part of the plan." Which of course couldn't be properly shared with him. So, Sally was involved but not involved. Just make up your mind. That's what he wanted to scream at the top of his lungs.

***

Warson Heights, Michigan. It hadn't been called that the first time she laid eyes on this land. Magisha kept the property after all these years. It was rented out a few times and updated to keep people from turning it into a historical landmark or something. It needed to blend in. People didn't understand why she kept so many pieces of property, especially this one.

She looked up at the tiny house and made her way to the porch stairs. Foolishly she forgot the keys, but it didn't matter. The Queen reached out her hand, which turned blue, the front door opened.

There was little to no furniture in the house. It needed to be dusted and cleaned desperately. That could be settled later.

"This is where it happened. It happened here... I know it happened. People can't tell me otherwise. I'm right. They are wrong. I'm right. They are wrong." She took a deep breath, "I'M RIGHT. THEY ARE WRONG!" She screamed at the top of her lungs.

She looked at the fireplace mantle. A mirror that was in desperate need of being cleaned was hung above it. She wiped it off and looked at her reflection, only she wasn't her. She was, but she wasn't. She was seventeen again; Seventeen and in love. Seventeen and pregnant; ready to live her life with the man she loved. Ready to be free of the social structure of English society.

Even though her parents had finally made enough to move out of Madeline's parents' house the year before she left for this new land, they were still considered poor by the standards of the day, Witch trash. That's what people in town would call them. It didn't matter what Madeline or her parents said, that is what people would call them.

He had promised to improve her life for the better. Magisha screamed again. She took the mirror and swung it across the room. It hit a wall and dropped to the ground smashing into a thousand little pieces.

"You just don't want to understand. You made me pay for his

crimes. You belittled me." Magisha was talking as if people were actually in the room. She then turned as if someone was standing right next to her, "Oh, you only married me to prove that I was wrong for leaving you in the first place... Joke's on you with the number of times I left you."

She then turned to the other side, "I'm responsible for your children hating you. I didn't force you to marry a scumbag, Maude!"

It was always her fault. It was never their fault. It didn't matter the crime. It didn't matter the circumstance. It was easier to blame her for things than it was for the people around her to take credit.

"I told you not to hire anyone without my approval. How did that work out, father?" she stomped her foot and moaned.

This was just upsetting her. Magisha wanted to be upset, though. She needed to be upset. In her mind, she was denied the chance to raise her firstborn child. She had to watch as those idiots screwed him up. They let him become a spoiled brat, and take up bad habits. When she knew the date of the *birth* was near, she had two choices; let it go or take control. It was apparent to the people around her that she was expected to take control always. So, why wouldn't she have befriended the parents of the child? Maybe she couldn't make certain choices for her son, but she was going to be damned if she didn't at least try.

The Gray Stone was always a backup in case things didn't work out. Oh, how they didn't work out. The boy was just like his father, if not worse. In the end, she would triumph because she made sure of it. There was only one option. Get rid of the boy.

***

"Remember, do not swallow the pill. If anything, we need to shove them in Blake's food or something," Sally stated.

Aarick seemed to be a little bit more himself since they came up with the plan, but she was not sure that he was completely back. She wasn't even sure that was at all possible. Aarick looked at her, "I know Sally. We have been over the plan." That was more in tune with the Aarick Langston she knew, loved, and feared.

The door opened, and Smythe walked in. He had the bottle that contained the binding potion. It was in capsule form, which was at least an improvement to the liquid version of the binding that Northland used to put on her telepathy. She understood why they did it, but at the same time, she was done being told that she wasn't allowed to be powerful. She couldn't help that she was presented with that power at her birth.

"All right," Smythe looked around. "Where is Blake?" he asked. Sally shrugged. He never came back after lunch. Smythe rubbed his forehead, "Great, well, it's time for your vitamins." He grabbed a white rubber glove from his pocket. Somehow Sally felt like putting it in his pocket, defeated the purpose of putting it on his hand in the first place. It didn't matter. Honestly, she was pretty sure they were eating magic-formed food, which meant they were malnourished. They got the taste, but none of the calories, which really made no sense in the long run with all the bizarre training, but again she didn't care. He came towards her with the pill in his hand, ready to put it in her mouth. She did, and she pretended to swallow.

"You know, Blake has been spending a lot of time away from the group as of late," Sally pointed out. Smythe stopped what he was doing and looked at her, "What exactly do you mean?" He asked. The young Magica girl frowned, "I'm just saying, I thought we were supposed to stick with the group. The three of us. Yet, he is never around."

This agitated the man. Sally had a feeling that it would. He handed Aarick his pill and ran towards the door, "I'll be back later," which meant tomorrow or a week from now or maybe five minutes from now. It was hard to tell.

The two children looked at one another. "He didn't even wait to see me put it in my mouth," Aarick said, confused. Sally spat her own pill into her hand and grabbed Aarick's. These are going right into Blake's next meal.

"Why are we making sure that he takes these again?" Sally looked him in the eye, "Do you honestly want him following after us? I think we have had our fair share of Blake Aldridge for a lifetime." Aarick nodded, "Ok, yeah, that makes a lot of sense."

There had to be something that would snap Aarick back into his old self. This was just not normal for him. "Do you remember the time you threw that party out in the forest?" Sally asked. Aarick started to laugh, "Which one? Oh, you probably mean the one where I tricked Maude in signing off on it, and Salloom was ready to go off on her for it."

Sally never thought it was possible, but maybe it was better for some people to be uptight and downright bitchy than it was for them to be nothing at all. Aarick fit very perfectly into that category. It was as if he had been given a lobotomy, and he was unsure how to be himself—a person who had never been afraid to be different and had always thrived on it.

"I know you think I'm being overly cautious, Sally. I can see it in your eyes. You just have to remember that there are things that I've seen and heard around here that make me hesitant," Aarick explained to her.

She felt bad in a way. She knew that he was subjected to weird one-on-one time with Smythe or other members of the WIA. It would not shock her at all if their motive was to brainwash and blackmail him into being whatever it was, they wanted him to be.

That part of all of this still confused her. The WIA was an organization that existed. They hadn't heard about it before the Gray Stone. It was clear that this wasn't an organization run by Magisha. If it was, then maybe this was what being a sacrifice meant, that Aarick was supposed to suffer at the hands of these people. If that were the case, she wasn't sure what it had to do with her.

Sally had always been rather indifferent towards Magisha. She was always on the younger side, and while she enjoyed tagging along with Mollie, Aarick, and Pepper, she was not actually part of their group. Whenever they got caught doing something they weren't supposed to do, she was never involved in things. In theory, there was nothing wrong with her until she tried to use Aarick as a sacrifice, she guessed.

Sally honestly didn't know how she was supposed to feel about certain people at this point. There was still the overwhelming question of whether her mother worried about her or cared that she had been unaccounted for, for this long.

***

At this point, Pepper had no idea how to react to anything. Her mother had hidden a twin sister from her, and her father's mother had some form of a phobia towards people from the Magic Realm. She also had to wonder if her father was even worried about her.

"Where is my body right now? Is father there?" Pepper demanded to know. Penelope looked at her, "I'm not really sure what is going on down there. Contrary to what people believe, we are only allowed to look after people connected to us, and since the Gray Stone, they have been very secretive and have stopped people from getting involved. The only reason they let me visit with you is because of the amount of time that you have been in your coma."

The lights started to dim. A candle blew out that was on the table. "What's going on?" Pepper asked. Her mother frowned, "I believe you are needed back on earth." She stood up and gestured for Pepper to take her hand. Pepper did, standing up and immediately wrapping her arms tight around her. This would potentially be the only chance she ever got to do this.

"I love you," Pepper said. She wanted to cry so much, but because of where they were, there were no tears. "I am so proud of the woman you are becoming. I can't guide you on what to do when you get back to earth, but I trust that you will be able to figure it out rather quickly," Penelope explained.

There were so many other things that Pepper wanted to ask her mother quickly. So many selfish questions, but she knew that her time was up. She looked up at her mother one last time, and the room started to fade. The unearthly fortress was no more; she was back on earth.

***

The red-haired girl opened her eyes. She looked around the room, "Where on earth am I?" This clearly wasn't a hospital. Pepper looked around the room and could tell that wherever she was, it was not well kept. There were things thrown all over the place. "Hello?" she screamed out. She was hooked up to a bunch of cords, but she felt fine. Pepper knew how to remove them. She read enough on comas to know what needed to be done.

The door swung open, "I swore I heard a voice!" Maude screamed." Pepper was both excited to hear Maude's voice but also confused as to why it was Maude's voice she was hearing. It only took a moment, though, for Maude and Professor Salloom to make their way over to her.

"Pepper, you are finally awake!" Salloom said, sounding very happy. "What on earth is going on? Where are we? Where is my father?" Pepper asked. Maude sat down next to her on her bed, "It was too dangerous to get into contact with him. Magisha knocked you out cold, and you were unconscious for over three years," Maude explained to her.

Pepper felt like she knew this but felt a disconnect between what happened right before she was in her coma, during her coma, and what was happening right now.

"I don't understand this at all," Pepper said. She hated not knowing things. Then it hit her, "Where is Aarick? Is Aarick safe?"

The two older people frowned, "We don't know," Salloom admitted. That was not what Pepper wanted to hear. She needed to hear that he was perfectly all right.

"We need to find him," Pepper demanded.

CHAPTER TEN

THE GREAT ESCAPE

Deep down, Aarick knew that Sally was right. It was not normal for him to act so defeated. It was unlike him to not demand to be the most important person in the room. Yet, it was easier to pretend that everyone else was right and he was wrong in this situation. However, he had just about enough of it.

"Tell me when you are ready to go," Aarick thought to Sally. Sally's mind-reading ability had finally returned to her.

"We just need to wait until they release us for our next meal. Then we make our move. We will go to wherever Blake has been wandering off to all this time."

Obviously, Sally was the brains behind this operation, and Aarick was perfectly fine with that. She seemed to have everything under control. He was just worried about what would happen if things didn't go the way she planned.

"I'm going to take charge in the next test," Blake stated proudly.

Aarick knew one thing very well. He was not going to miss Blake Aldridge. If there was ever a moment where he deserved to be able to say I told you so, it was regarding him. Blake was an asshole, plain and simple. He couldn't be trusted, and he was obviously part of this plan to kidnap Aarick. Whether or not it had anything to do with Sally was another question altogether.

The real question that Aarick wanted to know was if the WIA and Magisha were both trying to kidnap and torture him separately. He had no idea why they would both be so interested in him. There was nothing of significance unless the end game was to get money out of his family.

Ryder Langston was not about to drop a dime on a hostage situation, though. They probably were unable even to contact his mother, which honestly wouldn't shock him. She didn't want to be a mother, and she didn't want to be a Langston.

Just then, the door opened, which meant it was time for a meal.

"You did slip the pills into his last meal, right?" Aarick thought.

Sally looked at him, *"Yes. Honestly, the amount we gave him was probably too much."*

That didn't really concern Aarick, especially if their theory was correct about Blake being part of the group that kidnapped them. If there were side effects to taking that much binding potion, that was something that Blake would have to deal with himself.

"Finally! I'm starving!" He screamed. He ran out of the room without even waiting for them.

"That seemed a little too easy," Aarick pointed out.

The Magica girl shrugged, "Let's take it as a blessing. Come on, let's make a run for it." He nodded and didn't hesitate to follow her. The broom closet was down the hall. They passed a few people on the way, but none seemed to be the wiser about what they were doing. He had a feeling that these people were as in on the plan as they were in terms of why Aarick was even here in the first place.

The two aggressively opened the door. "All closets double as elevators!" Sally screamed at the top of her lungs as she slammed the door shut. Aarick had to admit the thrill in all of this. Suddenly, the door opened on its own. It had been so long since he had cast any spell that he forgot the door would automatically open. They were now in a room that appeared to have been abandoned.

Sally looked at Aarick, "We are free!" she shouted. Thank goodness, although he knew there were still obstacles ahead, though.

There was a bed in the room and a few random pieces of furniture, none of which had been dusted in maybe fifty years, if not longer. There was something about the air even outside of the dusty room.

"We are clearly in the Human Realm," Aarick pointed out. It just had such a similar aroma. He was about to say something else when a small thud noise happened downstairs. The two looked at one another and decided to investigate. The hallway of this house was not very long. It appeared to have three bedrooms and a bathroom that Aarick was afraid to explore. It wasn't as if they would be staying here long. He knew very well they were still on the run.

As they made their way down the stairs, he was ready to fight. Then he realized who was downstairs, and once again, he was ready to fight, "Kensington?" He looked at Sally with confusion. Why on earth was Kenzie Kensington here.

The dark-skinned girl jumped up from the couch she had been sitting on. She sort of tripped, "Aarick Langston? I thought you were dead! Welcome to my humble abode!" she giggled. Sally was the one initiating the weird look now, "Why are you here?" the Magica girl asked. Kenzie found her balance with the help of the lady who was with her, "Oh, that Blake Aldridge boy has been keeping me up here for the last few years."

There was a lot to unpack there but what Aarick heard first and foremost was that it had indeed been a few years. "What year is it?" he asked. "Oh, 2009!" the other woman said.

It had been almost three years. He was actually in some weird building supposedly in space for over three years… Three long years of his life. He would never get that time back.

He took a deep breath, "Who the heck is the chick?" Aarick snapped. There was a return to form for him after this confirmation and realization.

Kenzie turned to the woman, "This is Sharrie. She is my new best friend. We've been inseparable the last few weeks."

Clearly, Kenzie was a victim of something. What? He had no idea whatsoever, which made him less sympathetic when he again reminded himself, he had been locked away with Blake Aldridge, doing test missions for lord only knows what. This angered him. This was ridiculous. This was…

***

All of a sudden, he was standing in Magisha's office. Gem was standing in a cage behind him. He was out of breath.

"I'm not letting you leave my sight!" Magisha screamed at the top of her lungs. Aarick tried to make a break for the door. Instead, Magisha came for him. He held out both of his hands, though, and a force shield appeared, stopping her from being able to touch him. This confused him to no end. How on earth was he making a force shield. It must have been a spell or potion. As soon as the shield went into full force, she was being pushed backward and flung into her desk.

***

...And just like that, he was back to the present.

He looked at Sally, "We need to find Salloom." It suddenly hit him that Salloom had come looking for him right before the Gray Stone started. He looked up at Kenzie, "Ok, well, we are going to get going." he stated. There was a part of him that felt like they should have offered to take Kenzie along. Then there was a part of him that remembered his childhood with her not so fondly.

***

"It's all so blurry. I remember certain things, but I don't remember everything," Pepper told Salloom and Maude. She remembered that night in the park and that Magisha had shown up. She remembered being worried about Aarick; however, it was still fuzzy as to why she was worried about him. Then, she woke up almost three years older. It was rather bizarre, and there was this sense that she forgot the in-between of that. Had there been more to this story? There had to have been. "I need to get into contact with my father," Pepper begged.

Maude looked at Salloom and sighed, "Honey, we want your father to know you are all right. We just can't release you to him right now. Magisha could be watching after him, waiting for you to show up. If you do, she can backtrack where you came from and find us." Pepper understood that in theory but still. "I get that you two don't want to get caught. I really do." Pepper admitted.

It was Salloom's turn to speak, which meant it was lecture time. Pepper normally was all for it, however, this was a lecture that he would normally be giving to Mollie, not her.

"It isn't that we are afraid of getting caught. It's that we have been searching for Aarick the last few years. A bunch of dead ends, but between making sure you stayed alive, the only other thing on our minds was trying to search for him and coming up with a cure to the Gray Stone," Salloom explained.

Pepper started to get restless in bed and needed to stretch her legs. Salloom was insistent that she needed to stay in bed because her legs might not be up to walking yet. Pepper was walking at six months and talking at a year. She wasn't concerned with falling over.

The red-haired girl got up. She looked around the room further and walked over to a desk where a potion lab was set up, "I'm going to need samples."

Salloom looked at Maude, "Pepper really just rest."

Pepper turned around, "I've done nothing but that. Someone go and get me samples." As the stand-off started between Salloom and Pepper, a scrying crystal started to move by itself on a map at another desk. Maude ran over to it. Pepper was a bit confused, "What's going on?"

Maude turned and looked at both of them, "This has a piece of Aarick's uniform attached to it. He's somewhere in Michigan, the Human side." All three looked at each other, "I believe that Maude should go and get him. Salloom, you and I stay here and work on the Gray Stone cure." She wasn't going to argue any further.

***

The Queen wandered into her throne room. She still went through with her weekly sessions of listening to people beg her for things, most begging for a cure to the Gray Stone, with a few trying to pledge loyalty. If they were loyal, they would have tried to find Aaron-Richard. None of them had. A few people came forward over the years claiming to have spotted him. Magisha knew these were all false claims because if they really wanted this to end, they would have actually gone about catching him.

She sat on her throne. She liked being in charge, at least in theory. Power was all she had left after all these years. The door opened. The Queen stood ready to attack because no one was supposed to be in here unless she said otherwise.

Magisha nearly turned white, "Hello, sister." It was Jeden. The Queen quickly ran in her six-inch heels across the long path to hug her brother, which he reciprocated, but it felt cold. "How are you here?" She asked him.

He wasn't smiling, "I've been sent at the request of some people higher up to talk with you for a little bit."

So, now there was a higher power trying to stop her. "That's a dirty trick on whomever it was," Magisha said, a bit thrown back. Jeden gestured for her to sit with him in a pew, "We have a lot to catch up on. I do want you to know that overall, I am beyond proud of you. I also want you to know that, unlike the others, I acknowledge the fucked-up shit that you went through in the past. However, also unlike the others, I must point out how you must take a small bit of blame because of how you have handled certain things since then," he said as he looked at her sympathetically.

Magisha sighed and turned away from her brother, "I'm not going to be tricked into giving up." This was ridiculous. Her own brother didn't understand the cause she had taken up. She turned back around and looked at him, "You remember what happened. No, you weren't there. You were smart enough to leave by then." She stood back up. Jeden did as well. "I regret not being there for you. I should have fought with you harder over him."

It was funny. Salloom and Maude used to tell her that early on. They should have fought harder with her. They should have tried to show her what was right in front of her. Magisha sadly knew what she was doing. All she wanted was to believe what was being told to her was indeed the right path. The moment she witnessed the first death in their friend group, she knew it was time to stop everything. People wanted her to take accountability for her actions. She did what she did, and now she was preventing it from happening again.

"I never should have given up my son, a child of myself and that monster. The prophecy is bound to be true. I went to the Faits, to those Seers, and even those Human fortune-tellers knew that I had made a giant mistake, giving up a child of that power and letting idiots raise him."

Magisha hadn't thought about things in the long run. She gave her child a binding potion, however, they only last for so long, as she witnessed firsthand when she went to visit the *birth* of her child. The baby didn't even last a week before it started to show signs of power. This was why she had to spend so many years watching over her child.

"You need to let the guilt go," Jeden told her. He wasn't gentle with her. Magisha knew she should let the guilt go. It didn't mean she would. "No, this is for the best. I want my son to see what kind of a mess his father could have made for the world," she screamed loudly. Her brother shook his head, "You don't seem to get it, do you? Magisha, you've already finished what your idiot ex-husband tried to start." With that, he turned into light and disappeared.

***

"Ok, I have no idea what we just saw, but we need to get the hell away from that," Aarick said as he marched down a sidewalk outside of what apparently was a townhouse. He took a moment to observe his surroundings. Aarick looked at Sally, "We are in Warson Heights."

This was perplexing. It was like he had only just been here a few days ago, but in reality; it had been a few years. He thought of Pepper and Mollie.

Sally looked at him, "Why on earth would Blake Aldridge have been keeping Kenzie Kensington safe in a townhouse in the Human Realm? What purpose does that serve to any narrative?" The two didn't even have to answer that out loud. Blake Aldridge was a complete nutcase. He did things because it gave him the thrill of being all-powerful.

"Let's just move on from that... If I survive the end of this, I'll come back and put her in a nuthouse myself, though I'm sure her parents would gladly do it themselves."

The teenage Witch had no idea where they were going to go. They had to be careful about using Magic. That said, Aarick also knew they would have to hide somewhere. Magisha was very clear that he was the key to things going back to normal.

He looked around, "It looks as though there has been damage done but nowhere near as much as I thought there would have been." All he wanted was to spend a day soaking in a tub with a thousand candles around him. He knew that day was far from happening anytime soon, though.

Sally walked a little further up. There was what appeared to be a school with a crowd in front chanting. "What is going on here?" They both looked to read what some of the signs said, *'Witches belong in Hell'*. That's what most of them said.

"Oh, great modern Witch trials," she said with a false sense of excitement. They looked at one another. Aarick sighed, "We need to keep moving on. They could recognize me." He was ready to start leaving when Sally stopped again, "Do you think Magisha has put my name into the mix?" It was in the way that she said it that took Aarick back a bit. As if there was some excitement over an all-powerful ruler of an entire universe wanted her as well. "It's possible, I suppose."

There was something off in general about the Human Realm, more so than in the past. Yes, Aarick and Sally were both used to a certain status quo of the Magic Realm; however, at least in Aarick's case, he knew this was not the same aura the Realm usually gave off.

The Gray Stone had definitely taken its effect on things, and it sent a shiver down his back.

"Where could we possibly go?" he asked. Just as he asked, a woman passed them and gave them a strange look. "It's him!" she screamed at the top of her lungs, "It's the boy that the Witch is after!"

The two Northland students looked at one another and started to run. The woman ran after them but was clearly on the older side, if not potentially weakened from the Gray Stone curse itself. People started to surround them.

"Stop this!" Aarick screamed. Sally grabbed onto his waist in fear. This was the first time that she had acted like a little girl in years. No one was going to touch a hair on either of their heads. "Get back!" he screamed at the top of his lungs, putting his hands out. As he said this, a force shield formed around the two of them. It only lasted a second, but it managed to knock the angry mob around them, at least five feet back.

Sally looked at Aarick in confusion, "Where on earth did that come from?" Aarick had no idea. He was reminded of the brief vision that he had just had. "I think I might finally have an active power." The angry crowd started to get back onto their feet. Sally looked him in the eye, "Well, you need to get control of that power rather quickly."

As he tried to concentrate, a portal opened, and a creature in a hazmat suit exited, "Ok, back off!" a familiar voice that Aarick could not place for some reason screamed, "The kids are coming with me. You can all go back to what you were doing." While he couldn't see her face, the woman was clearly looking at the two of them. Aarick looked at Sally, "I think it is safe?" he spoke.

Sally sighed, "So, long as this isn't the WIA or Magisha, I suppose." The two ran towards the portal and jumped through it alongside the hazmat lady.

All of a sudden, Aarick and Sally were standing in a very disorganized living room with a potion lab set up. He could hear a shower going upstairs. "Ok, who are you?" Sally said, standing in front of Aarick. The little girl who had just needed his protection returned to being the fierce young warrior he had been spending much time with. "Oh, will you kids relax? It's just me." The woman took off the mask, and it was revealed to be...,

"Maude!" They both screamed at the same time. They rushed over and hugged her. "I had to put on a getup so that Magisha wouldn't recognize me if she showed up."

This was the first time in years Aarick finally felt safe. He felt back in his element. He had Maude back. The boy never realized how much he missed her until he finally saw her again after all this time. It was only then, though, that he really started to think about a few things.

He turned to Maude, "Do you know where Mollie and Pepper are?" Maude sort of looked happy and sort of looked sad, "Pepper's been here all along. Mollie, we have no idea what happened. The real question for us is where you have been." She picked up a bottle of water and started to drink from it.

Sally now started to rub her head, "We somehow ended up being kidnapped by some organization called the WIA." Maude dropped the bottle of water onto the floor, "Oh good lord, not that terrorist organization."

It really didn't shock Aarick that Maude would call The WIA a terrorist organization. "You realize that Dean Smythe was a member. Blake Aldridge, the kid he had rooming with me, seemed to be a member beforehand too." He was forced to room with a terrorist by a terrorist. Then to put it into further context, he had spent the better part of his life looking up to a woman who wanted him dead.

The former secretary sighed, "Well, that doesn't shock me. Smythe was a Northland student, and I remember him always being rather bitter," Maude explained. This sort of threw Aarick for a loop, "Smythe, of all people went to Northland? He gives off such poor people vibes." Sally laughed, "That's the Aarick Langston I know and love!"

Everything was becoming rather coincidental. The sound of the shower stopped, and he heard footsteps. He turned towards the staircase. Wearing a bathrobe with a towel wrapped around her head, Pepper walked down the stairs. "Aarick?" she said with the biggest smile on her face. He didn't even hesitate. He ran over to her, "Pepper, thank goodness. I honestly never thought I'd see you again."

Pepper continued to smile, "I just woke up from a coma." She just sort of blurted out. Pepper had been in a coma while he and Sally were kidnapped and held hostage. "Where on earth is Mollie?" Aarick lamented out loud. They all turned to Maude. "I don't know. I have to believe she is alive, but the fact that I haven't been able to scroll for her has worried me."

CHAPTER ELEVEN

MAGICA

Months had passed. Years really. Mollie Magica was sick of being a cat. She was sick of listening to Magisha ramble about absurdities. This was never going to end. Mollie had always looked up to Gem, but it was only now that she realized Gem was not a powerful Witch.

There had always been a sense of envy over the Princess of the Realm. Gem had everything that Mollie wanted; money that she didn't know what to do with and a sense of being untouchable, which yes, being Larissa Magica's daughter did have, but Larissa was also a laughingstock amongst certain circles because she fell for Zeus' tricks. It was Octavia Kensington who made sure to make this notorious amongst those in the know.

"Is there any chance you know some sort of Black Magic? I mean, I know it's forbidden, but it could get us released," Mollie pointed out as she looked up at Gem, who kept trying to shock open her cage. Gem looked down at her, "Mollie, if I do that, then I forfeit my immortality.

You know that very well." Mollie did. She also knew that she missed indoor plumbing and people food.

"I don't think you want to leave this office. I think you want to stay here forever out of fear for what your sister has caused." Mollie turned around and instantly felt bad about what she said. "It's not that I'm afraid of what she has done, it's knowing that it's probably ten times worse than either of us realizes. She has the Human Realm US government trying to invade for non-existent oil. Not to mention that every Human nation probably has attempted to find Witches to use as weapons in their armies."

Mollie had not even thought about it that way. It was one of those rare occasions where she admitted that maybe it wasn't a bad thing to think for five minutes. Mollie never really thought of her childhood back when she was at Northland. It was just easier to put her head in the clouds and pretend like everything would be all right in life, which it was. She knew she would eventually find a husband who would take care of her. She knew that regardless she would have a prominent education on paper even if she never actually took advantage of it. She could just follow in her mother's footsteps from a career standpoint if need be. Yet, thinking back to how things had played out over her life so far, there were times when she was frightened for what was to come.

The Magica household was an ever-expanding property purchased by her mother and her missing husband when they first got married. The rumor was that her husband had not been wealthy, which is why her mother kept her last name even though her family had disowned her. She knew that she could be successful and that the Magica name would only help her. Mollie had to admire that her mother was indeed successful. However, she also acknowledged that her mother was not a great mother, which was sad to admit.

The door opened, and Mollie looked up and saw that it was Magisha. "There has been a sighting! After almost three years, there has been a sighting! Aaron-Richard lives!" she cackled as she said this.

Mollie turned to Gem, who looked stunned and bewildered. "Are you sure it was actually him? You know very well that crazy people always spot him at malls and in the forest, and then it turns out to be a rock or an Elvis impersonator," the Princess tried to point out. Mollie hoped for Aarick's sake that this was true.

Magisha turned to her sister, "Nope. It was indeed Aaron-Richard. There were people who took pictures. Someone rescued him with a Portal. Probably a damn WIA member." Aarick was alive! There were so many emotions to be had in this. "The weird part about it was that he was spotted with the younger Magica girl. She's definitely grown. I guess that's nice. I find it odd that she would be with him. My gripe was never with the Magicas." She looked down at Mollie, "At least neither of those girls."

That was an odd thing to say, but at the same time, there was a sort of calmness in knowing her younger sister was alive and well. Of course, she would follow Aarick. She always followed Aarick. Aarick always insisted that Sally tag along, and Mollie always told her not to listen to him. Those words would never come out of her mouth again. Mollie owed the world to Aarick now.

"Was Pepper with them?" Gem asked. Magisha sat down at her desk, "No, but I'm pretty sure Maude and Salloom have her. She's definitely not with her father. That girl is definitely book smart, but I don't see her as someone who would be able to survive in the world by herself." Magisha looked down at Mollie. "Now that one..., there is a reason she is a cat right now... she could figure her way around. That's why I never urged her to go to class. The last thing someone with potential needs is an education. That's the last thing anyone needs."

***

Sally Magica was more than glad to see Maude and Pepper. However, with Pepper back in the equation of Aarick's life, it seemed that she once again instantly took a back seat. It had only been a few hours, and she understood that it was a long time since Aarick had seen him, but Pepper, even being in a coma, had not been humbled. There was no asking about Sally. It was all about how Aarick was doing.

Sally still felt that Pepper had feelings for Aarick. She also still felt that Mollie would be the better match for him. However, she did not want Mollie to be with Aarick for Aarick's own sake.

"I think we need to take a step back and try to figure out why you specifically are the target," Pepper explained. She turned to Maude, "You must know something." Maude frowned as she sat down in a chair, "All I know is that she was developing a curse, and Aarick was needed in some way. That was the reason she made sure you went to Northland." Aarick looked confused, "The reason I went to Northland was because Kensington didn't get into Orion Oakland and Magisha offered her a spot, as our parents didn't want to separate us."

Maude shook her head, "No, Kenzie is a legacy Orion Oakland. Her father and grandparents went along with her two brothers. Why would they not allow one member of the family in, especially when two other members were still attending." That was the first time that Maude had ever said something that really made you think. It was also kind of shocking to realize that Magisha manipulated so many behind-the-scenes things. "You knew all of this and never told us?" Aarick asked, a bit offended.

As he said this out loud, Sally did have to admit it was jarring to put together. Maude once again frowned, "Salloom, Gem, and I were all made aware of things on the surface. Salloom and I agreed, probably into your second or third years at Northland, that we would do everything and more to keep you safe when the time came. Do you really think it is normal for the secretary of a Queen to be friends with a bunch of school kids?"

Sally thought that was a good point, "Well, yes and no... I just always assumed that Magisha was making you keep an eye on us for our parents' sake." Maude's expression made it clear that they knew what she wanted to say, but she didn't want to say it because it could hurt their feelings. Aarick's parents didn't care. Larissa never showed up to the school. Sally wasn't really sure what kept Pepper's father away, but he never inquired what was going on.

"You kids were definitely the mischievous bunch. Early on, yes, we did have a protocol of calling up your parents, but as time went on, that just got thrown out the window." Maude admitted. Sally honestly was not shocked at the fact that none of their parents seemed to care. Again, it was odd that Pepper's father never seemed to come around. Larissa was definitely not about to deal with any of her children's bad behavior.

Her older siblings, even older than Mollie, were never known for being bright stars and pupils at their schools. Larissa never did anything about it. She honestly doubted that her mother would even care that Mollie probably went to class a whole twice a year.

***

"*I'm not mad,*" the boss explained to Smythe. This shocked the hell out of him. He honestly thought that this would be the death of him.

"So, then you don't want me to go and find them?" He asked. He really hoped that The Boss wouldn't want this because he was honestly sick out of his mind of dealing with that little brat Sally. Aarick had been easy to detain once they had their way with him. Sally, on the other hand, was much stronger than she looked.

"*It's all been part of my plan. We kept them far too long, to begin with. The next phase of the plan is ahead of us.*"

What on earth was the next phase? Smythe spent a year and a

half of his life dealing with Aaron-Richard and his misbehaved friend group. Then it was almost three years of dealing with him and that Sally girl. There was also the fact that he was instructed to raise an orphan boy in the form of Blake for the last fourteen years of his life, which made little to no sense to him in the long run.

Smythe hoped that whatever the next phase was, it would be the final one. He couldn't take any more of this.

The WIA needed to take power of the Magic Realm. That was the end goal. That was what he signed up for after he graduated from Northland. He was promised that Magisha would be thrown out of office. Smythe had never liked her. He didn't really remember her from his youth or his time at Northland, which had always struck him as odd, but then later learned she hadn't even been there. She had been running around the Human Realm while she let her curse brew. This was why he was a devote member of the WIA. They stayed on top of what the crazy Queen had been up to. The things that the WIA had on Magisha would shock her followers to no end.

There was a knock at the door, and Smythe could sense that The Boss had taken leave. "Come in." He knew who it was. "What do you want, Blake?" Even if the boss claimed that they were not upset with Aarick and Sally escaping, they would still most likely blame Blake, which meant that Smythe would have to take at least partial blame himself as his guardian.

"I just can't believe they were able to escape past us. They knew better," as Blake started to bang his fist on Smythe's desk. This kid was starting to become an even bigger burden than he already was. "You are the reason that they were able to leave. You do realize that, right?" Smythe asked. The teenager just shrugged, "I just don't see it." Blake said this with a smug look on his face. As much as he didn't want to admit it, Smythe realized that The Boss was right. Bringing Blake along with him back to the WIA headquarters was a very big mistake.

Blake had decided to take vengeance on Aarick for being smacked across the face once three years ago. He craved getting to be in charge. Smythe might not have been fond of Aarick himself, but the WIA and, more importantly, The Boss wanted him for the organization.

***

"We will have to figure out a way back into the Magic Realm without alerting Magisha right away," Pepper explained to Aarick and Sally. Sally again didn't really know why Pepper was taking charge of the situation, at least in terms of what Sally's role had been in the escape. Yes, Pepper was indeed a very smart girl. Sally didn't think she was jealous and yet had to evaluate why on earth she definitely felt spited by Pepper right now and a little bit by Aarick.

"I think you are forgetting a giant step here Pepper," Sally sighed. She couldn't believe she actually spoke to Pepper that way. All eyes were now on her. "We can't just go back to the Magic Realm and attempt to defeat Magisha without having a cure for Gray Stone." She made a really good point. Score one for Sally and one less for Pepper. What was the point of lying to herself? She was happy to know that Pepper was alive and well. She just wasn't thrilled about things going back to the old way so quickly.

"I agree with Sally," Aarick said. Maude also nodded. "The girl has a point. Magisha always has a fallback plan for everything. She might be whacked out, but she has a plan for everything." This dumbfounded Pepper for a moment, which made Sally a little bit happier than she should be. "I just want this to be over with," Aarick admitted. It was the way he said it, though. What was being over with going to look like?

"Will we go back to Northland when this is over?" Sally asked. She looked directly at Maude. "I mean, if the alumni board chose to keep the school open, I suppose. I'm not really sure what is going to happen to Magisha exactly." The way Maude said this was just frightening. A world in which Magisha was not in power. A world where Magisha was... Sally had spent so much time thinking about a world where Aarick could be dead, that she never thought about a world in which Magisha might be. "Could Magisha be captured?" Aarick asked out loud.

The front door opened. Salloom walked in, "It would be very difficult," he explained. He then tumbled onto the ground. The group quickly ran over and helped him up.

"I had no choice. I had to make sure we would be able to test Gray Stone from both a Human and Witch perspective. I thought there was a chance I had it before. I now indeed have it."

He started to become very pale. It was as if all the color in him disappeared for good. He looked directly at Pepper, "I... Need... You... To... Take... Charge... Of... The... Experimenting..." Pepper nodded and took a bag that he was hardly holding up. It contained blood samples in it. Sally assumed they were from Humans. It was so weird to see Salloom after all this time. Pepper walked over to the table where Salloom appeared to have been working on the experiments before. She turned and looked at Aarick, "We may have to collect things from the Magic Realm." Aarick was helping Salloom get onto a bed that was in the middle of the living room, "If it means ending this once and for all, then that is what we will do."

***

"So, Sharrie and I went on a walk today. It was pretty fun," Kenzie said to Blake but was still looking at Sharrie. Sharrie looked to be in her mid-thirties, slightly overweight, with extremely curly red hair. Blake was not entirely sure what Kenzie Kensington, of all people, saw in her. All he knew was that this was just weird to watch. "Ok, but what you are saying is that you did see Aarick here earlier?" Blake asked yet again. Kenzie took a moment to answer, "It's hard to say at this point."

This woman was driving him up a wall; both of them were.

Smythe walked out from the kitchen, "You've been hiding Kenzie Kensington in this house for how long exactly?" Smythe asked. Blake turned to him, "Since day one. Stop acting like it is a big deal." Kenzie started to stretch, "I'll have to show you where I live one day Sharrie. You'll love my house." Smythe continued to give Blake a look of complete disapproval, "You're telling me that you let this girl go completely *Gray Gardens* in a house with some strange Human?"

Blake wasn't sure how many times he would have to tell Smythe; he had nothing to do with Sharrie. He wished that Sharrie would go back to her burnt-down house and stay there. "I don't have to explain anything to you." Blake spat out. Smythe went to grab him by the neck, but he quickly scooted out of the way. "Kenzie was just about to tell us about where Aarick and Sally went," Smythe looked at the girl.

"Oh, I have no idea where they went. Aarick gave me this really weird look, said a few bitchy things like he always does, and then they ran out of the house."

Smythe grabbed Blake by the arm and took him outside of the house. There were several Humans who had been infected by Gray Stone wandering around. A mob of people had gathered across the street in a field to go after Witches. Smythe did not seem to be bothered with this.

"If you wanted to get busy with the Kensington girl, that's your business. That said, you can't hold up the daughter of one of the wealthiest Witches in the world for your own enjoyment."

Blake had no idea what he was talking about. At least he was going to pretend he had no idea.

***

Once again, the coast was clear as Magisha went to discuss things with the supposed military team she had put together. Mollie quickly ran over to Gem's cage, "We need to get out of here now. Aarick and Sally are alive."

Mollie didn't know how they could help either of them but knew that they needed a warning. Three years of listening to Magisha's ramblings had to be of some service to them. Mollie knew Aarick. He always had a plan for everything, and in the off chance that Pepper was around them, as much as she hated to admit it, she would help orchestrate a plan.

She looked up at Gem, "We have no choice. I'm going to have to resort to dark Magic." Gem looked defeated. The Princess looked at Mollie, "If I go missing, Magisha will only search harder. If you go missing, she might have a few people on the lookout, but she will just think of you as a cat still." Mollie wasn't really sure where Gem was going with this. *"Humanum illa erit!"* the Princess screamed from inside the cage. She repeated herself several times over. The room started to shake. Mollie started to feel very lightheaded as smoke started to form around her. She closed her eyes, and after a minute or so, the shaking stopped.

As the blonde girl opened her eyes, she was no longer looking up at Gem but was standing face-to-face. Mollie held out her arm and looked at it. There was no fur. Mollie was a Witch again, no longer a cat. "I thought you said you couldn't turn me back into a Witch?" Mollie asked. Gem sighed, "As I said, I resorted to dark Magic. There is a spell for everything in dark Magic. You need to get out of here now quickly." It was great to be back in her body. However, Mollie had no idea where to go to start looking for Aarick or Sally. "Where do I go?" Mollie wondered. Gem looked like she was trying to think, "Go to the Human Realm. Scry for Salloom. All I know is that Salloom and Maude intended to go to the Human Realm. Even if Aarick and Sally are not with him, he is sure to know how to go about finding them."

Being in The Human Realm all by herself, especially in this state after all that had gone on here, was not good. Mollie was both nervous and excited at the same time. "Thank you. Are you sure you cannot come?" Mollie asked. Gem shook her head, "Like I said, if I go then, it will just cause Magisha to be on the hunt even more."

Mollie reluctantly agreed. Still, it was hard to leave Gem here. "Hopefully, we are all reunited soon enough," Mollie said. She wanted to hug her friend. Gem put a melancholy smile on her face, "Just promise me one thing. Stop pretending to be an airhead when this is over. Be the best version of Mollie Magica." Mollie nodded in agreement, but in her mind, that version was still the best version of Mollie Magica. If Gem could make a sacrifice, then maybe it was time to examine a few things.

CHAPTER TWELVE
CAN'T GO BACK

After a while of Sally and Pepper budding heads over many vast subjects, Aarick and Maude silently realized it was best to separate the two.

Salloom was now in his room upstairs, resting. It was bizarre to realize just how much Salloom and Maude were sacrificing for him, really. It was also obvious, though, that they played a larger part in this ordeal than maybe they were being given credit for, which in theory, he didn't mind. At least he was used to this. People around him tended to not be the most honest in their approach to things.

He was still unsure of how he was supposed to tackle his memories with Magisha going forward. He now knew that there were motives behind everything that she did. Yet, he could still look back at some of those days and feel gratitude and happiness associated with them. At the same time, he could now add layers to those memories, that he never noticed until now.

The Langston child sat down next to Pepper at Salloom's desk.

She turned to him, "It almost feels like being back at Northland." She smiled. He knew that this was meant to be a fond memory for her, yet Aarick didn't know. "I suppose we will never go back to Northland." Aarick admitted. This made Pepper's smile drop, "I don't think that's the case."

Aarick knew that Northland had essentially been the only home Pepper, and even Sally had ever really known. Yes, they had houses and rooms within those houses, but they didn't spend much time there. During the Summer holiday, Aarick would go home for less than a week before he'd end up calling Pepper or Mollie to go on some bizarre adventure together. Nothing on that level occurred over the last few years or current. Just three wealthy children, getting into things that they should never have in the first place. This could realistically be the last time that Aarick and Pepper were ever together for a long period of time.

"I can't imagine that your father would want you to go back to Northland when this is over. I wish we could get in contact with him, so he knew you were ok." He thought for a moment and wondered why he didn't feel the need to extend that to his own parents as well. Then he realized they had the means to find him and protect him if they had wanted to. No member of the Langston family had been on his trail.

There was a glass look in Pepper's eye, "I think I remember something from when I was in my coma." Aarick turned and looked at her, "What do you mean? Do you remember overhearing something that Salloom and Maude said?" Pepper shook her head to say no, "More or less, I know this sounds strange, and maybe it was a dream, but I feel as though my mother came to me, and we had a conversation."

Aarick had never really asked Pepper about her mother or her father, for that matter. He had just assumed that if she wanted to say something, she would have. Aarick himself rarely discussed the Langston family, mostly because he was seldom ever around them. Mollie and Sally were a different story. It was hard not to be around

Magicas. Their mother was rarely discussed and extended family not so much, but they often ran into other Magicas on school holidays and even around town.

"It's weird. It wasn't like I was asleep for all that time. It was more like a state of meditation where I was able to not think, which is not like me at all," Pepper explained.

For as long as Aarick had known Pepper, he knew that she was not one to 'not' use her brain. She always had to be doing something that would stimulate her mind. He never saw her watching TV. Yes, she would sit down and be around it, but she was either reading or doing something else entirely while it was on.

"Then, suddenly, I went from having nothing on my mind to having my mother there. However, the moment I woke up, it was as if I forgot everything we spoke about, even though I feel like it should have been important."

He knew where she was coming from in theory—the concept of being able to spend time with a loved one missed. Yet, for him, that just wasn't his reality within the Langston family. His sisters were semi-close with one another as far as he knew, but at the same time, he also knew that they would probably grow distant as they grew older. His father didn't speak to either of his siblings. Aarick seldom saw any of his cousins. Their mother's family was even more mysterious.

Aarick wanted to say something encouraging to Pepper, "I am sure that once things calm down, you will have a chance to really think about things and make sense of the conversation."

***

It was nice to know that as much as Mollie and Sally claimed to have nothing in common, they shared one trait: a disdain for Pepper, which Maude did not encourage in the slightest. However, it was interesting to note; the former secretary could easily tell that Sally needed to be separated from Pepper before any real arguments went underway. Mollie would have used ignorance and the attention of Aarick to win any argument. Sally, on the other hand, was not afraid to use intellect.

"I just don't understand why she thinks she gets to be in charge. I am the only reason we escaped from the WIA," Sally said as she sat cross-legged on the ground in a field. Maude thought it was best that she got some fresh air. "Aarick and Pepper have been friends for most of their lives. It was bound to happen that they would want to catch up."

In some way, Maude understood where Sally was coming from. There were times in her friendship with Magisha where they would spend long periods of time together and be happy. Then suddenly, Magisha and Salloom would fall back in love, and Maude became the third wheel. It had been a while since this was the case. However, she still had memories of this.

It was hard to say if Maude could claim resentment towards Salloom or not. It wasn't as if she had a crush on either Salloom or Magisha. If Maude honestly thought about it, she just didn't like it when people would prop Magisha up as being right. Magisha knew how to get Salloom to side with her when she wanted. Yet, when she grew bored of him, she knew how to make him turn on her. Maude realized that thinking about Magisha was probably not for the best right now. At least not trying to think about her in a way that would make sense of her bad behavior.

"Tell me, what would you do to end all of this?" Maude asked. It wasn't lost on her that she was asking a child how she would end a curse. However, she and Salloom had yet to figure it out themselves. Sally looked up in the air, "I wish I knew. We need a cure for Gray Stone. She only used the Gray Stone curse to make sure no one got in her way with capturing Aarick," Sally explained.

She was correct. That was the only reason that Magisha had cast the spell. Magisha didn't like Humankind. However, it had nothing to do with why she wanted Aarick. At least she didn't think it did.

***

"Hello, Aaron-Richard!" Magisha said with a smile on her face as she entered his dorm room. He must have been around seven or eight when this had happened. Magisha remembered it very clearly.

Aarick turned and looked at the Queen. "Are we spending the day together?" the Queen asked, as she smiled at him. "We are indeed." Aarick said back.

The Queen had promised to spend the day with him. He begged her for months, but she had been busy with many tasks. It was so unlike her not to want to spend time with the boy. "We will do whatever you want today. It is Saturday, and we both have the day off. Maude has been instructed to hold all my calls. Salloom was instructed not to bother me." Aarick jumped out of bed, "I want to spend the day in your office!"

Magisha looked at him, confused, "Young man, I am the Queen of the Magic Realm. We can easily do anything in the world, and you want to spend the day in my office?" As she pointed this out, Aarick seemed to make this face as if he was disappointed that she hadn't noticed it the first time around. "I want to be just like you when I grow up. How can I be like you if I can't learn from you?" It was that line... Oh, Aaron-Richard...

***

The elevator door opened to the lobby of Magisha's office. She blinked and was back to the present date.

Aarick had been such a sweet child, as sweet as one could be, given his overall upbringing. It didn't matter. There was a difference between being a great influence in a child's life and being the one who was responsible for raising the child. Magisha was going to have her child back. She opened the door to her office and walked in. Gem was sitting on the floor of her cage.

"Oh, stop being dramatic," Magisha said as she walked towards her desk and sat down. "I can confirm that Aarick and Sally were indeed spotted in the Human Realm. I do believe we are nearing the end of this," Magisha told her much younger sister. Gem looked directly at her, "Do you even have a cure for Gray Stone?" The Princess asked. Magisha rolled her eyes, "Why do you care? It isn't like you are affected by it." Gem started to laugh. She stood up, "So, then you don't have a cure. You're going to capture Aarick and do what with him? Lock him in a room as you have done with me? It's too late to mold him into your image. If that's what your intention is."

At times Magisha wished she had left Gem at Northland. She would have been less intelligent taught under some of the hacks that she had hired there. "I intend to sacrifice Aarick for the greater good of the world." At least, that was what she had been telling people.

Once again, Gem started to laugh, "If you had wanted to sacrifice the kid, you would have done it when he was a baby. It would have been easier to do; you wouldn't have had a bond with him. Killing him as an adult would only harm your own mind. He would be at peace in the afterlife. Or worse for you, be a ghost that would haunt you for the rest of eternity."

Magisha took a deep breath. Her sister had no idea what she was talking about. "So, maybe I don't intend on killing the kid. Is it really a bad thing that I would want to make him in my image? You have no intention of ever being Queen. You've made that clear. Aarick is going to be a powerful Witch one day." At least that was what every Magical creature had told her that she had ever spoken with about him.

"You have how many children in the world? Why can't one of them take over? On that note, why does he need to be captured for you to mold him into a proper leader?" It frustrated Magisha to no end when people tried to question her motives. Aarick needed to be freed from the Langston mindset. People needed to think he was gone. The Langston family might not have been nurturing, but they had their own intentions for what Aarick should be. They wanted him to be the next in line to run the Langston Brand, which wasn't a bad thing. It just would undermine Aarick's potential.

The biggest mistake was to let Aarick spend time with Maude when she took him off to Hollywood to be in that Soap Opera. It gave him ideas that were not in line with what he needed. The Queen knew that with her influence and her influence alone, Aarick could be the perfect successor for her. At the end of the day, it should be her firstborn that was her successor, especially if Gem had no desire to ever step into the role. "One day, Gemma, you will understand why I did the things I did. You will thank me," Magisha explained.

***

What on Earth was Mollie doing? She didn't know the Human Realm well enough to be able to orchestrate it. Hallowton and Warson Heights were nothing alike, even if they were in the exact same place on a map. The blonde girl was free for only half an hour, and already she felt like she was in a lost cause. Gem forgot a few simple things. Mollie didn't have access to a scrying crystal nor a map. She was sure she could find a map if she really looked, but scrying crystals were harder to find, especially since she had no concept of the Human Realm's Witch community.

A small part of her wanted to reach out to her mother. Let her know that she was ok. The other part of her wondered if Larissa even realized she had been turned into a cat by Magisha. For all Mollie knew, she was not even missed, which didn't make her sad, at least not for the reasons she should be. As she walked down the sidewalk, she could tell damage was done. At least she assumed it was damage thanks to the Gray Stone. Mollie knew that Warson Heights was far from the nicest place on the planet, but she didn't know it was ever this distraught. Houses were burnt down, and buildings were boarded up. The Gray Stone curse had infected many people.

What confused her was why people would choose not to stay inside. Gray Stone was caught breathing in the air. If they had stayed inside and only exited, when need be, then they would have stayed normal. It was obvious from the amount who were infected running around, that the Humans had not grasped this.

"Mollie Magica?" A voice that sent a shiver down Mollie's spine said. She turned around. There was no way that it could be whom she thought it was. It was. "Kensington?" Mollie said in shock. She was standing feet away from Kenzie Kensington, who was wearing what looked to be a potato sack. Her hair was a mess. There was a woman next to her who looked even worse. "Where on earth did you come from?" Mollie wondered. The arrogant Kensington girl smiled at Mollie. "We have actually been staying at that condo. Sharrie and I, that is," Kenzie explained as she looked at the other woman.

In a perfect world, Mollie would have a camera right now. She needed to stay focused. "This is a crazy shot in the wind... have you seen Aarick or Sally or Pepper for that matter?" Mollie couldn't help but be in complete shock over what she saw from a girl who wore designer everything because she had always wanted everyone to know she was just as rich as Aarick. "Aarick was here the other day along with your little sister. Haven't seen Pepper in a couple of years."

Mollie was still having trouble processing this. If anything, it was best for her to just walk away. She didn't really know what to say to Kenzie and didn't have time to point out that she had clearly lost time in that the Gray Stone hit. "There you two are," another voice said. Mollie didn't recognize it, but she did. Then she spotted a vaguely familiar face. "Blake Aldridge?" she said in confusion.

This was all getting extremely confusing. Why on earth would Blake Aldridge be anywhere near Kenzie? He clearly didn't like her when they were back at Northland. "I'm so glad that you are ok. I looked for you," Blake explained. Mollie was confused yet again. Why was he looking for her? "Do you happen to know where Aarick, my sister, or Pepper are?" As he gave her this look of guilt. "Unfortunately, they ran off. Well, Aarick and Sally, that is. I really don't know about Pepper. Aarick was doing great; we became so close. It really hurt when he just decided to run away." Mollie tried to make sense of this situation a bit more.

"Are you implying that Aarick Langston was living with you and Kenzie along with whatever the heck that lady is?" Mollie asked as she pointed directly at Sharrie, who was now chasing a bird. There was a slight chance that what appeared to be a pigeon would be dinner for these three. Blake shook his head, "Well, Kenzie and Sharrie live in a townhouse that I found for them. Aarick and your sister were staying with Dean Smythe and me."

Mollie looked at her wrist, pretending that there was a watch, "I need to get going." The moment Blake mentioned that Aarick Langston was willingly staying with Dean Smythe, she knew very well something fishy was going on. On top of it, Blake had found shelter for Kenzie, independent from wherever Aarick and Sally were staying, which in theory made sense. Aarick couldn't stand Kenzie. In execution, Aarick was not that heartless. He wouldn't deny Kenzie's survival. Blake was up to something, and she really didn't want to stick around to figure out what it was. Blake, however, decided to run after her.

"Wait! You should really stick with us for the night. It's dangerous out there." The blonde Witch remembered taking pity on the boy back when they were at Northland. He was cute but not someone she would have regularly fallen for. It was clear that, as usual, she had made a poor judgment call. Pepper would never have let her live this one down. As much as she hated to admit it, she needed Pepper right now.

*****

"In theory, if we can find a cure, then we would essentially be in the clear," Pepper pointed out.

Aarick didn't think that it was going to be that simple, though. He just didn't want to point it out to her. However, he knew Pepper well enough. There was no way that she didn't realize this already.

"I just don't want anyone getting their hopes up. Just because we can counter with a cure doesn't mean I'll be safe, and that Magisha would be hauled off. Magisha is beloved by many people. I doubt that she is without supporters that would help deliver me to her."

It wouldn't shock him either if people just assumed that he was in hiding all this time. If he hadn't been kidnapped, then he probably would have tried his hardest to hide. Up until a few hours ago, he hadn't even realized he had an active power. He turned to Pepper, "You will never guess what happened a little while ago. I was able to create a force shield." This seemed to get the redhead's attention. "Without casting a spell, you finally have true active power. It seems a bit bizarre about your first power but even still." It was times like this that Aarick wished that Pepper could just congratulate him.

The door opened. Sally and Maude walked back in. Aarick hoped that Sally had blown off a bit of steam, but he had a feeling that the natural disdain the Spellington and Magica girls had towards each other would continue rather soon. "Any luck with the cure?" Maude asked. Pepper shook her head, "I got a little distracted talking with Aarick." Pepper thought for a moment, then she looked at Maude, "Do you know if Magisha based her version of the curse directly off the original theory of the Gray Stone?" Maude looked a bit confused.

"I mean, while she bragged about it constantly, she never actually explained anything," which was on-brand with Magisha. Aarick knew that all too well. She would constantly tell Aarick how he needed to take her word for certain things, which he did, and normally it worked out, but that only worked because he thought of her as a mother figure at the time. It wasn't like he even knew what his own mother's eyes looked like.

Aarick pounded his fist onto the desk, "What on earth did I do to her?" He really wanted to know. Magisha had been a constant in the young Witch's life, more so than his own parents. It drove him insane almost to realize that Magisha didn't actually care about him. She wanted him dead or something, which was clearly not going to be to his benefit.

CHAPTER THIRTEEN

A REVERSE TO A CURSE

"**S**o, then you have been living here?" Mollie looked around the townhouse. It was beyond filthy, and the blonde girl had a very hard time believing that Kenzie was staying here willingly. Yet, she seemed rather happy in comparison with the Kenzie Kensington she had known for years. Kenzie was not known for roughing it. Mollie wasn't either, but Mollie would have bitched and moaned from the start. Kenzie appeared as if everything was perfectly fine, "I like it here," Kenzie said as she continued to play cards with Sharrie, the middle-aged woman whom Kenzie apparently was best friends with.

Mollie turned to Blake, who had continued to look at Mollie non-stop since they sat down. "What exactly are you looking at?" she asked him. Blake laughed, "Oh, it's just you have great eyes," he explained. The blonde Witch had all the information she needed about this situation. Blake had been holding Kenzie captive in some capacity, but Kenzie clearly was not aware of it.

Kenzie somehow met this Sharrie woman, and Blake was not happy with it. Aarick and Sally were here, but somehow Mollie doubted that Aarick Langston actually slept or spent a prolonged period of time in this house. Kensington might have bitched and been over the top under normal circumstances. Aarick would have made a giant ordeal, and the universe would have known. So, while she did believe that Aarick and Sally had been here, she knew that there were bits of information not being shared properly.

"Well then, I better get going." Mollie stood up. Blake took her hand. She had a feeling this was going to be an issue. "Wait. You don't have anywhere to go," Blake insisted. The pink-loving blonde girl started to laugh, "Ok, now you've forced me to have to think." She then got right in Blake's face, "I don't like having to think," she stated out loud.

"What's wrong?" Blake asked, trying to sound like he cared. "I've been trapped in the form of a cat for the last however many years listening to a woman who I actually used to like, ramble about how much she hates my best friend. Also, a bunch of stuff about foreign policy that unfortunately I'm now well versed on."

She once again tried to yank her hand away from Blake, "Just because I play dumb blonde doesn't mean I'm stupid enough to give your sorry self a chance." Blake immediately let go of Mollie's hand. He started to hold on to his right arm and then started to shake both hands. His entire lower body started to freeze. It took all of ten seconds, and the only part of his body that did not freeze was his head.

"What did you do to me?" he asked. Mollie once again started to laugh, "Oh, you thought I wasn't powerful. I suppose that's what you get for judging a book by its cover. That's why I don't read books. Now I can easily reverse this before actual damage is done to your body. The question is do I want to?" as she looked at him with the most serious face the young Witch had ever given anyone. "I think you are confused," Blake stated.

Mollie rolled her eyes. She realized that Kenzie and Sharrie were still playing cards or didn't seem to care about what was going on right in front of them, which, again, was a giant red flag which this little punk wanted her to ignore. "I'm going to give you until the count of three," Mollie stated. Blake was already breathing very heavily. It was as if he wasn't even trying to fight back. "Ok, please, I'm begging you. I'll do whatever you want," he explained. She blinked, and his body instantly defrosted itself. She once again got right in his face, "Where are Aarick and my sister?" she demanded. Blake was trying to catch his breath, "I honestly don't know. They were with me at the WIA for the last few years, but they escaped a little while ago," he explained.

What on earth was the WIA? Mollie was getting nowhere here. "I want to see my sister!" She screamed at the top of her lungs. Kenzie finally looked over, "Do you mind being a little quieter?" She asked. Mollie finally snapped entirely. She walked over to her long-time rival, "Kensington! Go look in a mirror. Your hair is a mess; you need a shower, and you are wearing a potato sack..., your best friend. Not that you had real friends at Northland, just a middle-aged woman who clearly has no friends or family who care enough about her to come looking for her! Wake your pathetic mind up and look at the situation you are in!" the Magica girl screamed at the top of her lungs.

"It's true I don't have any friends or family who would come looking for me," Sharrie said, shaking her head in agreement.

Kenzie looked at the woman. It was almost as if she was looking at this woman for the first time. Kenzie looked down at what she was wearing. "What the hell has been going on?" She yelled, as she jumped up from her chair. It was obvious, at least to Mollie, that Kenzie finally had a wake-up call. It was still unclear as to how Kenzie, of all people, would fall for this. Then it hit Mollie... Kenzie was desperate for compassion and someone who would care about her. Mollie almost wanted to hug Kenzie.

"You evil little conniving sneak! How dare you let Mollie Magica make sense!" Kenzie screamed even louder than Mollie had just belted out. Mollie then came back to reality. She still couldn't stand Kenzie. Mollie started to rub her forehead, "Ok, well, I'm off now. Have fun amongst yourselves." Mollie walked out of the kitchen into the living room. She thought for a moment about where she could go from here. It was then she remembered something; "The statue of liberty."

***

Pepper looked through an old spell book. It was practically useless. Then, she made the foolish mistake of attempting to look up the Gray Stone on the Human internet. It definitely popped up, but it was just a giant dump of Human Realm conspiracies. This was not working.

The redhead turned to Aarick, "The only way we are going to find a cure is if we have the actual ingredients to the curse she originally put together." This meant one of two things. The redhaired Witch assumed that Aarick could peace them together. The boy sighed, "Well, we can't time travel. The only other option is for one of us to go and collect a sample of the Gray Stone itself, which would mean going into her office."

It would appear they were in an all-losing situation. Yes, they could go to the office. However, there was not much hope that they would actually get what they needed, as they would probably get caught.

"Is there any chance you could try and control your visions?" Pepper suggested. Aarick pondered over the suggestion, "I've tried in the past. They are just too random. Plus, over the last few years, my powers were bound." It was as if the universe was against them in this situation. Then it hit her, "Astral projection!" Pepper jumped up from her seat and walked over to a bookshelf. Salloom, of course, had a book about how to channel different powers. She flipped through it until she discovered a page on the subject matter.

"Perfect. Well, if you can master it," Sally walked back in from outside. "Master what?" she asked, annoyed. Pepper had a feeling that the young Magica girl was angry with her for some reason. Sally needed to get over it quickly. "Pepper was just discussing Astral projection as a way to get to the Gray Stone."

Sally rolled her eyes, "You want Aarick to transport himself into Magisha's office?" The way she said this, Pepper had to admit sounded bad. "He wouldn't actually be in the room. Just his essence. However, if he can channel things properly, he should be able to grab a piece of the Gray Stone when he teleports back," Pepper explained.

It was obvious that Sally was about to retort. Pepper really wished that the little girl could be more like her older sister. "I'll do it," Aarick said, stopping Sally from speaking. Sally looked at him, very annoyed, "You are going to risk your life for a stupid Stone? Let me do it. She has no use for me." Pepper wasn't exactly opposed to this at this point. Aarick put his hand on Sally's shoulder, "I know you want me to be safe," he explained. It offended Pepper that Sally thought she assumed she didn't want Aarick to be safe. "You've been yelling at me for the last few years, though. When was I ever safe? Obviously, the curtains have been raised, and we can see the strings attached," the boy explained.

"So many sick games needed to be addressed," Pepper thought to herself. The fact that they never got into trouble was now making a lot more sense. Mollie, never having to go into class, and how Magisha didn't care. She just wanted Mollie around for some reason. Aarick went to look at himself in a mirror. Pepper had to admit that he had definitely grown more so into his looks. She needed to stop looking at him like that in this serious moment.

The male Witch turned and looked at the two girls, "Pepper, teach me how to astral project."

***

"I know you are up to something," Magisha told her sister. She threw a bottle of water into her cage.

If there was one thing that Magisha knew, it was that Gem was great at keeping secrets. Gem had always wanted a puppy, but Magisha hated animals. Gem was secretly able to get at least a dozen or so dogs past her over the years in their penthouse. Magisha always assumed that Maude helped her do so. Maude really was an incompetent secretary, sadly.

"Ok, what is the secret?" Magisha asked as she sat down on her couch. Gem looked at her in confusion, "I have no idea what you are talking about," Magisha sighed. The girl needed to learn to tell the truth once and for all. Gem shrugged. It was rather annoying to see her act this way. The Queen had been rather good to her younger sister the last few years. She was never in any real danger, and she never allowed herself to be in danger.

"Where are our parents?" the Princess asked. Magisha was actually thrown off by this, "They are somewhere safe. That's all you need to know," Magisha stated. Those two idiots... She rolled her eyes just thinking about them. The last thing she wanted to think about were the Stone parents.

"I mean, you just assume that they would feel something about the fact that their daughter has caused this much destruction," Gem pointed out. The girl was fishing for answers, but Magisha wasn't going to budge. Eventually, Aarick would be caught, and she would be free to raise her son the way she wanted. However, the last thing she needed was for Gem to go running off to find their parents.

"Find something else to dwell on, little girl." Magisha said very sarcastically. "What does killing Aarick Langston even accomplish?" Gem asked as she sank to the ground of the cage. Magisha turned to her and was a bit confused, "I never said I was going to kill him. I said I was going to sacrifice him. There is a difference." She couldn't have the boy known as Aarick around if she was going to finally raise her own son. The two could not exist at the same time. At least that is how she saw it. Aarick was a creation of bad parenting and poor choices from those idiot parents. Her son needed to be re-educated on his beliefs and how he saw the world.

The younger sister started to rub her forehead, "Do you ever make any actual sense?" Gem shrieked. The Queen was about to respond when she heard a noise from the West Wing. "What on earth?" Magisha said to herself. She looked at Gem, "I will be back."

The Queen turned around and opened the door that led to the secret wing. That was definitely not a normal noise; at least not one that she would hear from inside a room that was not supposed to regularly have people in it.

There was something about this situation that made Magisha get a bit nervous. She immediately started to speed up as she walked up the spiral staircase that led to the West Wing. The door was not opening. This made no sense. She held out her hands and pushed the wind, which caused the door to slam off the hinges and onto the ground.

Finally, it was all too perfect. She was finally face to face with him, "Aaron-Richard." For a moment, her heart melted. She remembered the boy that she had accidentally grown to love. Then she remembered his upbringing made it impossible for her to raise her son in this world. It was him, but it wasn't him. "I knew you would eventually turn yourself in." The queen laughed.

He just looked at her. There was fear but also anger in his eyes. She knew him so well. She knew almost everything about the child. "Why on earth aren't you speaking back? You are never this quiet," Magisha stated. There was something off about him. More than just the fact she had been searching for him.

"Why did you do it?" Aarick asked. The Queen rolled her eyes, "Why did I do it? You just don't understand, my child. It had to be done. You are more powerful than you realize—the ability to see the future and the past. You tread the thin line of being a Good Witch. I had to stop you from turning evil," Magisha stated, which was the truth. She did not want Aarick to make the same mistake that her husband had. Though in her husband's case, he had always been evil, at least from the time they had met.

Aarick was a blank slate; a slate that Magisha could help clean and craft into the most powerful Witch on the planet. "We could be amazing together. A true Witch Dynasty," Magisha explained to the teenage Witch. This made the child stare blanky at her once again, "Amazing together? You told the world that you want me to be sacrificed! You want me killed, and you are still not giving me a clear reason," Aarick explained to her.

He fell to the ground and started to shake. He looked up at her, "You just don't understand. You were the mother I never had. You were the reason I stopped begging to go off to Orion Oakland every year. You treated me like your own. Then suddenly, I'm enemy number one," he explained to her.

For a moment, she felt bad, but she couldn't let her guard down with him. She knew from experience that Langston's were excellent manipulators. "I'm sorry you feel that way, but I'm just doing what is good for everyone around you, including yourself." She went to get closer to him, but as soon as she was close enough to his wrist, the boy disappeared. "The universe wants to see me pissed off! That's what this is. Magisha screamed.

***

The address appeared to be correct, but Mollie was honestly not so sure. She had only been to Pepper's house once, but that was done so by the portal. While they were there, Mollie refused to go outside, and Aarick had his own reasons for refusing to leave the house. Here the Blonde Witch stood, though, in front of a harbor as she looked out onto the water and saw the Statue of Liberty.

Pepper often claimed that Mollie was over the top and trashy. Yet here she was looking at the home that Pepper happened to live in. "How on earth am I supposed to get over there?" She looked around. There were infected Humans as well as ones that had not been infected at all, who were going about business as usual. Mollie was definitely in New York City.

Across the street, she happened to notice a broom resting against a shop front. Mollie realized it was incredibly dangerous to ride a broomstick in plain daylight with all the Humans wandering about. However, what other option did she possibly have? A portal would not work for anyone who was not a member of the Spellington family. She needed to get into that house. The Spellington's were the only Human Realm Witch family she knew of who would have access to a scrying crystal.

Pepper might be there. Then again, she might not. She might be with Aarick and Sally, or she might not. Mollie had no idea. All Mollie knew was that this was her last-ditch effort. If this didn't work, then at least she would have a place to hide out for a while. Mollie and Pepper might not have labeled themselves as friends, but she couldn't possibly imagine that her father would turn her away.

The blonde marched across the street as she saw an infected Human start to attack a group of Humans. Mollie decided to look at the situation like this; she could use her powers to stop them, but the Humans were technically innocent. Mollie couldn't just harm someone, and while the infected Human might cause harm to the unaffected, it wasn't her fault that those Humans didn't just stay inside.

Mollie grabbed the broomstick. It was far from riding grade. It was gross if she were honest, but beggars couldn't be choosers. She preferred to ride side saddle as opposed to sport style, as it was less awkward. The blonde Witch focused. It had been so long since she had ridden a broomstick. Brooms were like bicycles. They weren't used as a form of transportation amongst Witches, so it wasn't as if she did this regularly.

"Um, ok broom… let's just get me to that island without falling into the water. We can do that." It wasn't lost on her that she was talking to a broom in the middle of the New York streets, but she was in New York of all places, and again there was an infected Human just down the street. She felt rather normal in comparison.

The broom started to hover. "Let's do this thing!" She started to fly. There were a few people who clearly noticed and started to shout at her. Mollie did not care, however. All she cared about was getting this over with. She needed a spa day. No, a spa week and then just endless hours of shopping.

The pink obsessed Witch started to bang on the statue. She had no idea how to access the Magic side of it. However, she knew very well that the Spellington family could see everything that the Humans did to their home.

"Mr. Spellington? Pepper? It's Mollie Magica! I'm the roommate of Pepper at Northland. Hello? Please, if anyone is there, please let me in. I need your help!" as she was mindlessly screaming. It was therapeutic or her after all that had gone on, including being ignorant of what was going on with her family, being a cat for several years, listening to Magisha ramble for hours and hours every day, and not knowing if Aarick was ok. She even worried about Pepper if she were completely honest.

Finally, a door formed in front of her. She immediately opened it and found herself in the grand foyer of a French-style mansion. "Mollie?" David Spellington asked the girl. Mollie had only met the man a few times but started to hug him. "Is Pepper with you?" He asked her. Mollie looked into his eyes. She was close to tears for several reasons. Yet now it was clear, Pepper was not here. "No… I have no idea, but I have an idea about how to find her," she explained.

***

The adrenalin was rushing through Aarick's body. He had no idea he would be able to astral project so easily. It came so natural to him. He looked at Sally and Pepper. Maude and Salloom were also there and looked to be angry. Salloom dropped to his knees as weak as he was and started to check his pulse.

"You... Should... Have... Not... Done... That..." Salloom told him. He was having trouble speaking. Aarick knew he shouldn't have, but he needed to. He succeeded. He held out his hand. He had a piece of the Gray Stone. "I saw her. She saw me. We spoke very briefly."

Pepper and Sally looked at one another, and even in their silence, Aarick knew that everyone in that room was both worried but curious. Maude then looked him in the eyes, "Was she ok?" Aarick was a bit taken back by this, but he knew where she was coming from. He knew extremely well. "No," he whispered. That was the truth. She was no longer the Magisha that he had known. However, that might have been the Magisha that Maude and Salloom had known. "I recognized her face, but I didn't recognize her at all otherwise. It was as if she were a different person," Aarick explained.

Maude's face fell... her expression was all he needed to see, that unfortunately, that was the Magisha whom Maude had known very well.

The Spellington girl grabbed the stone from Aarick's hand. Sally and Maude helped Salloom get back up and sat him down next to Pepper at the lab that he had set up. "It might take a little bit longer, but more or less, we should be able to backtrack this curse with the actual stone and Salloom's blood samples," Pepper explained as she looked back at the rest of the room.

Aarick couldn't help but smile. He got up and walked to the staircase to sit down. Maude walked over and joined him. He put his hand on her own, and they looked at one another. "Maybe there is a way to defeat her without harming her," Aarick said. It shocked him that he would say that, but it was truly how he felt. Through all the bad that she had caused, a small part of him hoped the way she was could be saved. Maude gave Aarick a hug, "No, Aarick, we are beyond that, unfortunately," she expressed to him.

If Maude, of all people, was acting as a voice of reason, he knew that, unfortunately, it had to be the truth. She was never that blunt. "How will we go about capturing her?" Aarick asked in genuine curiosity. He had an actual plan about how to go about capturing the most powerful Witch in the universe.

Maude pushed her hair out of her face and sat up a bit, "I have an idea, actually. Salloom might be a bit reluctant to it, but I think I know what needs to be done." There was finally a sense of an ending to things. Aarick was grateful. He got up with the intention of helping Pepper but also to keep the redhead at arms distance from Sally. However, as he did, a portal formed in the room. Aarick immediately formed a force shield for himself and Maude.

"Get over here quickly!" he screamed at Pepper, Sally, and Salloom. They ran as fast as they could, but a person started to walk out, a familiar person. It was her... "Oh no..." Pepper said with terror on her face. "Oh, I've missed you too, roomie!" Mollie said as she exited into the portal, rolling her eyes.

Aarick quickly dropped the portal and ran over along with Sally to hug the blonde Witch. "I've missed you so much. You don't even know," Aarick explained. Mollie smiled, "Same," She admitted. Sally looked at her, "It's good to see you," as she hugged and wouldn't let go of her big sister. "It's good to see you as well. I don't think either of us ever thought we'd admit that out loud," Mollie explained and gave her a little wink.

Mollie then looked at Pepper, "It's actually good to see you as well. All of you," she said as she looked around the room. Pepper said nothing but nodded. Aarick cleared his throat, "So, then I think it is time we take our lives back."

PART THREE

2002

"Just relax for five minutes, Salloom," the Queen told her husband. He had just spent hours yelling at her, and for once, she let him have his way and just go on and on and on. It was honestly the most annoying thing on the planet to listen to his nagging. Almost as annoying as listening to her teenage sister or Maude's ramblings.

Maude was too busy being vested in those God-awful daytime soaps, in any case. Vivica, this and Luke that, just complete and utter nonsense, and a waste of time. However, Magisha had to admit they kept her distracted, so she couldn't complain about them that much.

She sat at her desk as Winston walked back and forth, thinking he was coming off as intimidating. He wasn't. However, the very smart but very annoying man stopped and put his hands on her desk. He knew she hated smudges. Regardless, he looked her right in the eyes, "I want you to give this up and move away with me," he bluntly said.

It took him hours to convey that. Magisha smiled at him, "Darling, there is no reality where I can step down from this position." She got up and walked over next to him, "I love you. I really do love you. I know I can be petty," she grabbed his hand. He was reluctant, but she wasn't really asking. "This job is like the mob. There is only one way out. Death…"

He looked at her for a long moment. Magisha was frowning. It was the truth though. If she had given it up centuries ago, it would be a different story. She had too many enemies, and she could never be a normal citizen.

"I don't want to be the husband of the Queen anymore," Salloom said, yanking his hand away from her. He grabbed his jacket off the couch and walked towards the door. "I'll see you at dinner... I guess." He looked at her one last time before leaving. He slammed the door behind him.

Magisha froze in place for a moment. Her blood turned cold, and she had goosebumps. This wasn't what she wanted. It was just the reality of the world.

There was also a matter of Aaron-Richard, or Aarick as he now called himself. If only she could just let him live his life. The life she had already planned out for him centuries ago. It just wasn't fair, though. She was denied the chance to raise her son. She was denied the opportunity to just be with Salloom, the man she genuinely loved and should have been with in the first place. She created a mess. It was a mess that she intended to fix. The Queen looked over at the door that led to the West Wing. "Almost..."

CHAPTER FOURTEEN

ONCE AND FOR ALL

Magisha stormed down the spiral staircase that led to the West Wing. She had just got off the phone after all was said and done with the Aarick situation.

She slammed open the door and walked over to the cage where Gem was. "Aperta!" the dark-haired Queen screamed at the cage, which opened at once for her. She looked at her sister, "So, then, where has Mollie gotten off to?" Gem clearly knew something. Magisha definitely knew she wasn't a cat any longer. "That girl can't even figure out the difference between geometry and geography. Do you honestly expect me to believe that you didn't do something to her?" Magisha demanded an answer from her sister.

Gem looked confused at this point but walked out of the cage. "I'm not even going to pretend," Gem said, looking at Magisha. "I helped her escape. I doubt she has gotten far, though. We both know what she is capable of." Magisha started to laugh, "You and your lies." The Queen yanked her sister's arm and walked into the lobby. Maude's

TV hadn't been used in quite a while. However, it would right now. She flipped on the TV and turned to a news station. There, a poorly filmed video of Mollie flying on a broomstick appeared on the TV.

Once again, the older sister looked at the younger one, "Would you care to explain that?" Magisha asked. It was clear that Gem was at a loss for words. "Let me keep you quiet for a moment. Aarick was in the West Wing for all of a few minutes. I think he was able to astral project or something," the Queen explained. She was getting rather sick of Gem's silence. "Will you say something?" Magisha spat out. Gem tossed her hair back. She then looked her sister in the eye and smacked her across the face. "What the hell have you gotten yourself into?" Gem screamed at the top of her lungs.

If Magisha was honest, she never thought that anyone had it in them to slap her. There was a moment of respect for Gem. Just a brief one. The Queen started to hover in terror over her sister. "How dare you slap me! I raised you! I kept you safe, and you slap me?" Magisha screamed.

Gem rolled her eyes, "First of all, sister dear, it's still up in the air as to whether you raised me or kidnapped me. Also, keeping me safe and holding me hostage are two very different things." Gem looked around the room, "Am I free to go or?" Magisha once again started to laugh, "Knock yourself out, kid. I tried with you. I tried with so many. If you don't want my help anymore, then fine," Magisha screamed back at her.

It clearly threw Gem off to hear this from Magisha, but at this moment, Magisha finally had enough. She finally had enough of everyone. "Goodbye," Gem spat out. She didn't look back as she walked into the elevator with her back to her.

"Well, that was the last of them," Magisha told herself out loud. "No more Gem, Salloom, Maude, or even Aarick. My parents and my children, well, that is another story altogether." The Queen then sat down at Maude's desk. She looked in a drawer, and there were, of course, tissues and most definitely, at this point, expired snacks. No office supplies whatsoever.

"Well, I know what is next. I've known for a while now." There was much to prepare for. However, Magisha decided to sit and relax for a moment longer. Just a moment.

***

"Ok, I've searched everywhere I could possibly search for Aarick. I'm honestly a bit concerned about Blake and his hostage abilities, though," Smythe explained to The Boss.

It took a moment for a response. *"How many times must I reiterate this? I do not give a damn about Blake!"* screamed The Boss. Smythe actually realized this greatly. However, he hoped that if he dragged out something else, The Boss would forget that he himself had screwed things up so badly.

"Apparently, the other Magica girl was spotted flying over New York today," Smythe pointed out.

"That's of a little importance to me. Did you at least survey the area? Check and see if Aarick might be with her?"

Obviously, Smythe had. He had just returned from New York, searching every corner of the city. "Well, I couldn't exactly find either of them or the Magica girl that we had with Aarick for a while," the agent told his Boss. The Boss stopped talking altogether. This was just wonderful...

***

Kenzie had Sharrie drive her car, as she tied up Blake in the back seat. He had not recovered very well from Mollie using her powers on him. In the right frame of mind, she had to question why on earth she had sat on a couch basically day and night for several years while Sharrie had access to a car. She had no clue where on earth they would have gone, but the Kensington money could have gotten them something better than this. Kenzie wasn't the one whom crazy Magisha had been looking for.

"Has my family looked for me at all?" Kenzie screamed at Blake. Blake was very hesitant to answer. She could easily tell. "Damn it," she said out loud. Kenzie knew the answer rather well. "Where are we driving to?" Sharrie asked her. Kenzie sat back and rubbed her forehead for a moment. Once again, she really had no idea. Then it hit her, "Sharrie, hold on for a moment." Kenzie needed to concentrate. She had to open a portal and get an entire car through.

"Damnare portal aperire!" Kenzie screamed. A portal opened in front of them on the road. They were probably about to cause some form of an accident, but when was that ever a concern of Kenzie in the past? The car sped through the portal, and they were now driving through a forest.

"Where the hell are we?" Blake asked in shock. Kenzie definitely didn't land where she thought they would, but it was close enough. She recognized the forest from her childhood. "Just keep driving in the direction you are going, Sharrie. Eventually, we will reach my house or Aarick's, but that's right next door. Mind you a few miles down."

Kenzie realized that her family had not missed her in all this time. If they had, then they would have gone looking for her ages ago. She wasn't an important aspect of their lives, which she was fine with. Kenzie was not exactly fond of her parents or older brothers, for that matter herself. It was time she got what belonged to her and started her life anew. She never thought it would involve a middle-aged woman as her best friend, but she clearly could not take Sharrie with her. Before Sharrie herself started to go nuts, it was obvious that there weren't many people who cared about her either.

Life was proving to be a wild ride for the Kensington girl. Wealth had clearly not worked to her advantage, at least not family wealth. This new life would be better. "Ok, why exactly am I here?" Blake demanded to know.

Kenzie turned and looked at the idiot boy again, "I'm kicking you to the curb the moment that I get what I came for. The only reason I took you was that you've proven to be creepy enough to follow me. So, I beat you to the punch and let you come along for one last ride," she spat out.

Kenzie once again turned around and looked at what was ahead. Ironically, it was the end of the forest and the beginning of the Kensington estate, which stretched about two miles wide. That was just the home alone. That didn't count the entirety of the land. "Home at last... one last time...," Kenzie said with the utmost certainty.

***

"It needs dragon scale. Plus, it will need some trace of Magisha's blood, which might be difficult to get. We might be able to get away with a close relative," Pepper explained to the group.

The redhead was able to break down the entire curse based on the ingredients the Stone was made from. There were definitely elements of the curse in Salloom's blood sample, but certain blockers were in place. "If it weren't for the fact that this behavior is not acceptable, I'd have to admit that the way she created this curse was rather ingenious."

This, of course, prompted a dirty look from Sally. Pepper was ready for Sally to be put back into her playpen. If she were being honest, as much as she was happy to know Mollie was ok, having the girl back just meant another person to babysit day in and day out. Aarick always allowed it. "We need to figure out a way to go about making everyone immune to the curse, though. It's not going to be as easy as just asking people to take an antidote," Aarick pointed out.

Pepper had thought of that herself. "I was thinking we make it airborn much in the same way that the original curse started. If we can make it air-born, then people have no choice." She knew the Human race would be extremely wary of anything that was given to them. The reality was that anything to do with Humans was better done with force, rather than giving them a choice.

Maude sat on the edge of the desk, "I am not in the mood to deal with the aftermath from the Council of Three," the former secretary explained. Pepper looked at her, a bit confused. "I don't think that the Council of Three would really care about this. I'm sure they want a cure just as much as everyone else."

Pepper spent little time in the Human Realm herself but knew very much about the Council. They were a group of three Witches from three different regions who were elected and replaced every hundred years. They were the rulers of the Human Realm Witch community and kept order between the Humans and the Witches. They were not particularly fond of Magisha and the Magic Realm from all the gossip she had heard about them over the years. Supposedly they felt it was unfair or possibly were jealous of how Magisha had kept power for so long. Which in retrospect, they might have had a point.

"The Council of Three are going to deal with it. They should have gotten involved years ago the moment they realized that Magisha was nuts," Aarick screamed.

***

As the Langston teen was working through his stages of grief, he was now at the point where he wanted everyone to take responsibility for their actions. He had already spent several years blaming himself for this. Aarick realized that he was not responsible. On the off chance that he somehow was, then he was not sorry for it.

"That woman taught me to take ownership of nothing I don't want to. I'm sure as hell not going to start now!" He screamed out of context. However, the looks on everyone else's face made it obvious they all knew exactly what he was talking about. Mollie walked up to him and put her hand on his shoulder, "I think things will all work out to our advantage. They always tend to work out for us," she pointed out.

It wasn't that Mollie was incorrect. It was the fact that there was context that needed to be given to what she just said, which excluded the fact that Magisha essentially always let them get away with everything. There was no Magisha to stand by their side in this case. "I can't believe I'm saying this, but I miss the three girls that were in my dorm," Sally stated and started to laugh. Aarick was a bit confused by this. The younger Magica girl always complained about how she wanted to move in with Mollie and Pepper. She hated the three girls in her dorm. "I'd love to answer the phone just one last time," Maude added as she too started to laugh. "Heck, I even miss giving lessons to a group of children who have no idea what I'm talking about," Salloom said.

It was great that they all had time to be nostalgic for a moment; Aarick didn't. The nostalgia he had was now mixed with this feeling of being lied to and years of 'did this really happen'? Well, sure it did, but why did it play out this way when realistically, it would have played out a different way for someone else.

The Langston child walked away from the group and went outside. He looked out into the sky, "Was I even really up there?" he asked out loud. "Yeah, I've been asking myself that same question a lot over the past few days." Aarick turned around, and Sally was standing there. "We will just have to accept that right now, as we are in a transitional period. What happens after that we will deal with when we get to it," the young Magica explained.

That was probably the best way to look at things. It was just hard to be in such limbo about life already lived and a life that had not yet been determined. "I think it is obvious that someone is not going to come out of this alive. We need to start thinking about it from the perspective that it could be me," Aarick told Sally. Sally started to become teary-eyed. Aarick kneeled down and started to wipe her tears, "We'll get through this."

CHAPTER FIFTEEN

FAIRWELL AND HELLO

It was the first time in years that Gem had been outside of the Capital Building. The first time in years, she had been outside of a cage. Her sister had left her inside a cage for that long. Magisha was never a particularly loving being, but the fact that she locked her up was starting to hit Gem in a way that she never thought it would.

The Magic Realm was in turmoil. Right outside the Capital Building, there were protestors. It would appear they were protesting Magisha. However, in reality, there were two groups of protesters, the ones who were for Magisha, and the ones against Magisha.

People were holding signs with Aarick's face on them with red x's over it. The same went for pictures of Magisha. The sad thing was she understood where the ones with her sister's face came from. She couldn't understand, even given the circumstances, where people would think Magisha was right in her misconstrued anger towards Aarick. However, she realized that whatever this misplaced anger was towards a literal child, it needed to end.

The Princess had no clue what would be next in her life. Would she finally go and try to find Maude and Salloom? Hopefully, they were with Aarick and potentially the others. She had friends in the Human Realm. If they were unaffected by the Gray Stone, she could technically go and live with, or at least be around them.

Gem never wanted to be a princess. Yet, she was one. In the Human Realm, she was a runway model who did some print work every so often. In the Magic Realm, she had people who would bow down to her. Yet, at this moment, no one seemed to notice her, which she was OK with.

The Stone sister walked onward and noticed the gates to Northland. Did she dare take a look at the school? It couldn't possibly still be running. There was no point. It was a part of her past that she would be giving up rather quickly. Gem knew it was time to move on. "I'll just spend some time in Europe," she told herself.

She was about to open a portal when she felt something brush against her leg. She looked down. It was a poor and defenseless dog, "Oh... look at you."She picked up the dog and held it for a moment. Magisha never let her have a dog. "Do you want to come with me? Get away from all the madness that is Magic and royalty?" The dog sort of just breathed heavily. The Princess shrugged, "I'll take that as a yes."

***

Kenzie managed to grab several bags full of clothes and other items. At first, she wasn't so sure she even wanted to take photos of her childhood or her family. Then she realized that one day she would want to look back. It definitely wouldn't be anytime soon, but maybe at some point.

Sharrie was in complete shock over the size of her house, which

Kenzie guessed was rather large. It was never something that she herself had paid attention to. Kenzie realized, though, that she would probably never live in a house as large as this one again. Did she ever really live here? Not really. She went to Northland during the school year. During the Summer holiday, she spent time in a completely different house or traveled with her mother, who never really seemed like she wanted to be around her. "So, where are we going?" Blake asked, annoyed.

Kenzie looked at him as she got back into the car, "We aren't going anywhere. You are getting out right here. What you choose to do is your choice. I'm done worrying about you," Kenzie explained.

In retrospect, this was her fault, and she acknowledged that. She was a bitch to him the first day they met. The one thing Kenzie was unsure of was whether or not this was the reason he played savior and captor towards her. "Have a great life," Kenzie spat out. Blake took his seatbelt off and got out of the car. He looked at her in confusion, "So, then where are you even going to go?" he asked. Kenzie shrugged at him, "I'll figure it out. For the first time in my life, though, it won't be at the expense of my family or Aarick Langston. That's for sure."

She looked at Sharrie, "Drive," she said. The car started to move, and Kenzie looked back at Blake, who looked rather confused, "Should we go back for him?" Sharrie asked. Kenzie shook her head, "Absolutely not. He is a part of the past. A past I want nothing to do with. We need to get out of here. The first smell of Human in the Magic Realm, and you will turn to stone."

***

This was no longer fun. The child had resurfaced and, of course, went missing almost as quickly. "Why did I think that anything would come of this?" Magisha scoffed. She was now talking to herself. "I should have made Gem stay. I should have figured out where Maude was. I need someone."

Magisha knew, based on her past, that just because Salloom and Maude were on the Aarick train right now that they would most definitely return to her at some point. Probably to plot against her, but at least they would be there with her again.

*****

It was just too typical that Maude would put Mollie in the same room as Pepper. Pepper was just in a coma, and now she was being further punished with the joyful love of being Mollie Magica's roommate again. "I'll take the bed next to the window," Pepper said. Mollie gave her a dirty look, "You had the bed next to the window at Northland." Pepper now was giving her a look, "Yes. I prefer to sleep near the window."

Pepper plopped down on the bed before Mollie could attempt arguing further. "It's going to be a long day tomorrow. We need to get the dragon's scale and plot a way to get Magisha's blood." Mollie now found her way to the other bed and sat down herself, "Oh, wow, I forgot what it was like to sleep on a bed." She slept on the couch the night before. Pepper found it just too hilarious that Mollie had been turned into a cat.

"How are we going to get dragon scale without going into the Magic Realm?" Mollie wondered out loud. Pepper started to lay down on the bed, "Well, we are going to have to go figure it out ourselves. I'm sure that we will be fine. We have active powers," Pepper pointed out. It always annoyed Pepper how powerful Mollie was, yet she never realized it herself. This very stupid blonde could take over the universe if she wanted, with just her powers alone, if she could figure out how to use them properly.

"I suppose you are right," Mollie said. Mollie supposed that she was right? She was always right. Pepper chose not to roll her eyes.

"Pepper?" Mollie said. "Yes?" the redhead responded. "I missed you. I was worried about you," Mollie explained. Now she felt bad for thinking all of that up. "I'm sure I would have missed you too. If I had been awake, that is."

This made Pepper a bit uneasy. She sighed, "Mollie, I feel like something major happened to me while I was in my coma, but I can't remember what it was for the life of me."Mollie turned to look at her in confusion and intrigue, "Well, maybe you should start writing down your dreams when you wake up. Maybe you will relive the dream and remember what happened," the blonde Witch stated.

It shocked her, but that was actually decent advice on Mollie's end. Pepper didn't know how to explain that it felt more like it was real life. Yet, it didn't feel like life at all. It felt so much more peaceful. Pepper knew that everyone was unsure about how to return to their normal lives, if and when this was over. Yet, out of everyone, she craved to have that sense of normality back, her normal, which meant being the smartest person in the room and people accepting it. It meant summers with Aarick or her grandparents. It meant seeing her father once or twice a year but loving every minute of it. Her father..., she missed her father so much.

"Have you attempted to make contact with any of your family?" Pepper asked as she started to lay in bed and look at the ceiling. Mollie was doing the same at this point. "No..., my mother probably doesn't even realize that I'm missing," the blonde explained. That hit Pepper a bit harder than she would have expected. Pepper had known Mollie nearly her entire life. She was not fond of her, and even still, she didn't really like her. Yet, here she was, feeling bad for her. "Goodnight, Mollie," she said. "Goodnight, Pepper," the blonde girl said back.

***

"Hey Langston!" said a boy who Aarick recognized..., but just

hardly. Aarick smiled, "Oh, hey," His future self said back.

"Are we still hanging out after class?" The boy who was tall with a button nose asked.

Future Aarick nodded, "Yeah. Totally." The guy walked away, and someone who looked a lot more familiar ran up in a rage. He realized exactly who it was.

"Aarick, we need to get back on track. You need to stop flirting with the Human boy and kick my sister out already," a future version of Sally demanded. She definitely was a few years older, and there was a bitterness about her. "Sally, we've been over this. We aren't going to kick your sister out. She needs a place to stay," His future self-explained.

Aarick recognized their surroundings. He had a vision similar to this already. They were in a building that looked like a rundown school, which made him question if he still went to Northland or not. Then it hit him; Sally just said the Human boy. What on earth was going in this scenario?

***

The Langston teen shot up in bed and started to breathe heavily. Sally was sitting on her bed reading over a spell book. "Oh, good, you are out of your vision," she said. Aarick turned and looked at her, "I just had this weird vision of the future. You and I were arguing at some school about some Mortal boy and Mollie," Aarick told her.

Sally nodded, "Yeah, that sounds like something we would argue about eventually," Sally said. Then, Sally's eyes lit up, "You said you had a vision of the future?" Sally jumped out of bed and went to look out the window. She then turned and looked at Aarick again, "A vision of the future," Sally said once again.

Aarick was a bit confused, "Yeah... I tend to have them if you remember," Aarick reminded her. Sally smiled, "Aarick, you had a vision of the future where you and I were there. How old did I look?" Sally asked.

"I suppose a couple of years older." The Male Witch explained. Then it finally hit Aarick himself. He jumped out of bed, "We are going to survive." That was definitely a vision of the future. He was going to survive this. They were going to survive this. He walked over to Sally and held her tight, "We have nothing to worry about," he told her.

Sally broke away, though, "As much as it is nice to know we survive, we still don't know how this will play out. We also don't know how far away that vision was. It clearly wasn't next week," she explained to him.

That was true. Aarick knew this was a touchy area for both of them. After being exploited and then kidnapped and harmed, the concept of being over was bleak. "I guess the question is, will we ever truly be done with this?" Aarick stated. Sally frowned and went back to sit on her bed, "I think we need to stop thinking about the past when we think about the future. It's a matter of moving on. The fact is that the days of you being queen bee at Northland are over."

It sounded harsher than it really was. Sally was one hundred percent correct. Even if they ended up at Northland or some other prep school, Aarick was never going to be looked at with the same essence that he once had. Those days were over. This was the last conversation he would have on that subject matter. He knew very well that his past would probably be daunting him for the rest of forever.

***

Maude panted outside of Salloom's door as she waited for him to open it. She couldn't take it anymore and stormed into him, putting on a shirt. "Maude!" He quickly screamed. "Oh, like I've never seen you naked before. I worked for Magisha for how long?" It was odd to speak about Magisha as if she was only an employer and not a friend.

She closed the door behind her and sat down on Salloom's bed without being invited, "It's the beginning of the end and the start of something new. How do you think this will play out?" she asked him with genuine intrigue as to what his response might be. "I think that life will never be the same for us again," Salloom said, looking her in the eye.

She feared he would look at her in the eye. It meant that he was indeed being honest with her. She absolutely hated that. "With Magisha, all the bad came with a sense of security. Whether it meant job security or knowing that we would have some misadventure to not look forward to, we knew where we stood. In the future, we can move on with our lives," Salloom pointed out.

A life without Magisha Stone. A life where Maude had to rely on her own self-worth to get through things. The former secretary didn't think that it was possible. Was it, though? She had been fine for some time now. The only thing was that deep down, she knew she was still letting Magisha pull some of the strings. "We could have moved on. We still could," Maude said, now not looking at Salloom. She could hear him make a sighing sound.

"I'm sure we could." He sat down next to her, "Heck, we could put a charm on Aarick and make him look like someone else entirely. Continue to stay on the run for a few more years and then resurface and claim that we adopted a child," Salloom told her.

She knew what he was doing. He was making up something so outlandish because he knew even, she would end up rolling her eyes. It worked.

"The days of Magisha knows best are over. The days of Maude and Salloom think for themselves are just beginning," Maude told him. Did she believe it? In time she would. There was a knock on the door. "Come in," Maude said. Salloom turned and looked at her. Maude shrugged, "What?" Salloom rolled his eyes. Maude realized it was his room but even so. The door opened and Aarick walked in. "I needed to talk with the two of you," he explained.

Maude had a bad feeling about this, "Aarick, I need to say something first," Maude explained. She stood up, "I'm sorry for not removing you from the Magisha situation sooner. You never deserved any of this."

Salloom stood up and touched her shoulder, "No. It's not Maude's fault. It's my own. I should have made your time at Northland so horrible that you demanded your father transfer you somewhere else." The professor explained.

Aarick looked at them both. Clearly, there was confusion in his eyes, and Maude could easily tell this.

"That's um…, thanks." Aarick rubbed his forehead, "I just wanted to let you know that I had a vision earlier. It wasn't the first vision I've had as of late either in this sense," the teenage Witch told them both. Maude was intrigued. However, she could tell in Salloom's eyes that he was confused. Aarick started to rub his neck. Maude noticed in the past that when Aarick was nervous, he would rub his neck or play with his hair. "You see, I have these visions of the future. I'm always in a hallway, just sort of standing there, and Sally appears sometimes, only she is clearly older." Aarick blurted to them.

"Oh, Maude, you were in one once." Aarick pointed out. Aarick started to think a bit, it seemed. "Anyway… I just wanted you guys to know because it's a sign that we all make it out alright." Maude looked at Salloom with the same reluctance in his eyes that she had.

The blonde woman walked over to the teen, "I mean, it's great there is hope in you. However, visions don't always turn out the way you expected." At least that was what Magisha would always ramble on about.

The issue was that in Magisha's visions, she only ever saw the past. It was sad to say, but Magisha's visions were also not the best judge of character. She would constantly remember things differently than they played out. Maude would try and correct her all the time. Salloom tried as well. It never stopped her from saying otherwise. "You just need to be careful," Maude hugged him.

Aarick quickly broke away from the hug, "I'm sorry, but every vision I've ever had has come true. I've tried many times to stop things that have happened in visions," Aarick told them both.

Maude realized what she was doing all of a sudden, "Oh, good lord," she looked over at Salloom, who was clearly thinking the same thing. She again looked at Aarick, "We've been gaslighting her for years, haven't we?" It was the first time that they ever said it out loud. It was the truth, though. The two of them, over everyone else in their lives, had gaslit their best friend. Well, his best friend. Salloom and Magisha's relationship was a lot more complicated.

"I should have just listened to her," Maude pounded her fist against a wall. Salloom quickly walked over, "She spouted as much nonsense as she did, in fact. I believe Aarick one hundred percent. Magisha, on the other hand, would interpret things in convoluted ways. Plus, her visions were even more random than Aarick's," he explained.

***

Aarick looked at the two older beings and was a bit taken aback. They were trying to justify treating someone who, up until a few years back, was someone important in their lives. He assumed that she would always be important in some way in their lives if he really thought about it.

"Why would you two choose not to believe her?" he demanded to know. It was very much old Aarick who was taking control of this conversation. Maude turned to him. She had these puppy dog eyes that made it hard to feel any sort of anger towards her. "She had an active imagination outside of her visions, especially when it came to things about the future. She can only see the past," Maude explained.

The blonde raised her finger to make a point, "You know, why would anyone want only to see the past?" Maude pointed out. Aarick wasn't going to deny that it seemed rather bizarre in theory, but it also would be helpful if he ever tried to hone in on the power better.

"I love you two, but you need to think before you do," Aarick rolled his eyes. If he was honest, it was rather sad that he felt like he was the only adult amongst two children. It wasn't even these last few days. It was back at Northland too. "Tomorrow, we need to sneak back over to the Magic Realm. It's the only way we are going to get dragon scale easily," Aarick stated.

"We should be safe from Magisha out in Dragon Country. However, dragons tend to be the most untamed of all creatures. So, this will be an interesting challenge," Salloom pointed out. Aarick had only ever been around one dragon. They did not get along. At least, that was how Aarick chose to perceive things. If Aarick did indeed live through this, which seemed like he would, he would make it a goal to believe people when they told him things unless it was Mollie looking for money. Lord knows that girl ended up with half of his allowance on more than one or two occasions.

CHAPTER SIXTEEN

DRAGONS AND POWER PLAYS

"I will not be giving in to your oil wants!" Screamed Magisha on the phone. She was about to yell something else but decided it was best to end the call there. The Human Realm proved to be as incompetent as it always was. The Queen could never understand the concept of giving Humans ultimate power.

She realized that the Council of Three were technically the ones running things, but it didn't change that those three idiots themselves allowed humans to be rulers of the land. It wasn't as if there was a Witch president for the Witches in the Human Realm. That would have been a conflict of interest on many levels. It would have given additional power to someone who knew how to use it, not just some idiot Human. It made her laugh. The Council of Three was more corrupt than she was ever accused of.

"Having fun being lonely?" a familiar but invisible entity asked. Magisha knew who this was, unfortunately, "Oh, good, you're still around."

She looked straight forward as if she knew that whoever it was, was standing right in front of her, "Are you still trying to defeat me?" Magisha asked. *"I don't have to. You're doing it by yourself,"* The Boss explained. The Queen rolled her eyes, "So, how is Smythe? You know he may have been the most incompetent of the Dean's I've hired since Northland has been open."

"How did you know about Smythe? There is no way you figured that one out on your own," The Boss spat out. Magisha could tell by the tone of their voice that they were not happy with this reveal. "He was a student at the school. I might not have been around for long during that period of time, but I still have access to records. He was a radical hater of me back then. He continued that well into his adulthood."

Magisha never understood what his issue was with the Boss. "I swear some students expect me to drop everything and be their best friend," the dark-haired Queen rolled her eyes again. Aarick was a different story. She had no choice but to let him warm up to her. If anything, he found it odd that they were so close, at least the older he got, and tried to avoid her. She blamed him being a teenager on that, though.

"Are you still here?" Magisha asked.

"Well, someone has to be. You're going mad by yourself," The Boss explained to her.

Magisha sat down at her desk, "I don't know who you are. While I have several guesses, I will say just this. You will never win against me. Even if on the off chance that I don't get what I want, I can take solace in knowing that you won't win," Magisha stated.

Years of battling with the WIA; always made her laugh, "You play terrorist leader for as long as you can. You will never win. I've made sure of that," the Queen said, knowing the irony in what she just said. At least she could admit it.

***

"I've been instructed to strip you of your WIA status," Smythe said as he looked at Blake. They were sitting in the townhouse together. "How on earth did you let the Kensington girl get away, and also Mollie Magica?" Smythe truly was furious. He had spent years training Blake to be smarter than this. Blake just looked away as Smythe spoke to him.

"Apparently, Mollie is a lot more powerful than anyone wants to give her credit for." Blake waved his hands in the air. This is why Smythe had trained Blake to look at every situation from at least ten different outcomes. People are unpredictable. Humans are typical with their behavior, but a Witch was unhinged. He should know that being from the Human Realm and being a Witch himself. Yet, Blake was power-hungry.

"You can't seek power. You have to let power come on to you. It's the only way that you will ever be successful at the WIA," Smythe screamed at him. Blake got up from the dusty couch that he was sitting on and started to walk around. "You are just such a typical authority figure," he looked at Smythe and smiled. "You know exactly where Aarick is, don't you? You've always known. This was always the plan," Blake screamed.

Smythe rubbed his forehead and stood up. He crossed his arms, "It wasn't my plan. It was the Boss's plan. If it were my plan, we would have overthrown Magisha far before it got to this point. The Boss wanted things to play out this way, and The Boss is the one who is in charge."

He knew that Blake didn't understand this because, again, he was not looking at things from a logistics standpoint. Smythe was not in charge of the WIA. He was an agent, a high-ranking agent but even so, an agent.

Blake started laughing, "You're a lab rat," he spat out. Smythe could see it in his eyes. He actually believed this to be the case. "Kid, you have a lot of growing up to do if you want to succeed in this world. The era of Magisha is coming to an end. Many changes are going to be made, and the WIA will be at the helm of many of them. It will be better for you to stay on our side than not." Smythe was proud of the WIA's work over the years.

***

"I don't understand why we can't come along?" Mollie said as she crossed her arms. Sally was glad that not only did Salloom and Maude state that Pepper and Mollie couldn't come along, but Aarick doubled down. They would have just gotten in the way. Aarick insisted that she herself go through which made her happy. This was as much her battle now as it was his.

"We'll be back in a few hours. You need to stay with Salloom and work on the overall batch." Pepper's antidote had somewhat healed Salloom, but without Magisha's blood and the dragon scale, he remained in no condition to be traveling.

Sally suspected that Maude was not going to be the best chaperone, but she insisted that she wouldn't let them go it alone, which the young Magica girl could respect at least on the surface level.

Dragons were interesting creatures. Unless you stole a Dragon egg and raised it yourself, the Dragon was unhinged. There were, of course, Dragon institutes where you could visit the civilized Dragons, but this group couldn't exactly be seen in public. "Ok, Maude, you need to stay on task while you are out there. Do not turn your eyes for one second," Salloom told the secretary.

Sally already knew that the only way this would end well was if they made Maude sit on the sidelines. "Aarick, you are going to have to rely on your new force shield power. It's the only active power you have, and Magisha won't be able to track it," Salloom told the Langston boy. Sally looked at Salloom and waited for him to give her instruction. He didn't, which kind of annoyed her. Who was she kidding? It really annoyed her. "Well, I guess we will get going," Sally said a bit loudly. "Ok, why does Sally get to go, and I have to stay?" Mollie put her hand on her hip as she said this. Pepper even sort of nodded in agreement. "I said so. That's why," Aarick explained.

It was weird to hear Aarick say something against Mollie or Pepper but in favor of her. She realized that it really wasn't in favor of her, but she was a participant in place of them for the first time ever. "Alright, let's get this portal going," Aarick said. He gave Pepper and Mollie a look to just let things go with the flow. Sally had to hold back a lot of dirty looks.

***

"Oh, dear lord, it smells terrible!" Screamed Maude the moment they walked through the portal.

Aarick looked around and had to agree that it did smell rather awful. It was so weird to be back in the Magic Realm. They were somewhere in the Eurasian quarter of the Realm, though. It wasn't as if they were familiar with it. "Are we in a jungle?" Sally asked.

Aarick turned to look at Maude because he had no idea. Maude had a puzzled look on her face as well. "I really only know this place based on the yearly visits Magisha would humor us in. We would not stay long."

Aarick did not see any dragons. It really just looked like an exotic jungle of sorts. He was sure that in the Human Realm, this land probably was a civilized country. Yet, there were trees and plants with a wet soil base, which Aarick had not been expecting. "Do we know where the Dragons are?" He once again turned to Maude. Maude looked around, "Normally, there are a lot more," she explained.

All of a sudden, there was a loud noise. The three Witches all turned around. There in the distance, two dragons flew by them. They didn't seem to notice them. Sally started to hold on to Aarick. "Sally, you have nothing to worry about. Dragons are a gentle species so long as you don't try anything." Sally looked at him, "So, they will be fine with us taking a scale?" Aarick had no idea. There was something off about Maude. She seemed as if this was no big deal at all. As if she was being put through the wringer.

"Are you ok?" he turned to ask her. The former secretary sighed, "Yes, this just reminds me far too much of the crazy nonsense that I've had to deal with because of Magisha. The reality is that this is because of her as well. It's just on the opposite spectrum for once."

Aarick found it so weird that Maude had been essentially a henchman to Magisha's craziness all these years. He didn't hold it against her. It wasn't like she had much choice.

"Oh, my goodness... Oh, my goodness...," Sally said in a puzzled voice. The Langston child turned, and a Dragon was brushing up against her. "Is that a baby?" Sally wondered.Aarick couldn't help but giggle. "It would appear to be," Maude said, shocked in tone. Sally dropped to her knees and started to brush up against it, "It's purple. She's so beautiful."

Aarick had to question how she knew it was a girl, but honestly, the more he thought about it, the more he didn't really want to know. The Dragon was brushing up against Sally, almost as if she was a cat. "Can I keep it?" Sally looked at Maude. "Oh, you want it now, but just wait in a few years when it is the size of a house." Maude pointed out to her. For a very brief moment, it felt like old times; Maude having to be a voice of reason when she wasn't great at it; Sally being a little girl; and Aarick not taking the world so seriously, yet it would only last a moment in time.

Maude kneeled down and started to rub her hand against the

Dragon herself. She was clearly feeling its scales. "Oh, you're a good girl, aren't you?" Maude asked. Sally continued to smile, "Can I name her Ainsley?" Sally asked. Maude shrugged, "You can name her anything you want, but we aren't taking her home." As she said this, she held up three dragon scales, "I think this should be enough for Pepper to extract. We need to get out of here before the mama dragon shows up."

CHAPTER SEVENTEEN

REUNION

The inclusion of the Dragon scale definitely did something. Now it was just a matter of getting Magisha's blood. Pepper had been up all night, ensuring that there was the right amount of each ingredient. "How do you do it?" Aarick asked her as he stretched.

Pepper couldn't help but look as his shirt rose up, revealing his flat stomach. She stopped looking before he noticed. "I don't know what you mean," she spoke. The Langston teen laughed, "How do you continue being so brilliant-minded? I mean, you are a teenager, and you know everything about everything," Aarick told her. Pepper couldn't help but blush. "I guess it's just easier to drown yourself in knowledge than other things," she explained to him.

The Langston boy couldn't help it if she wanted to stay shopping or look for new boy toys like Mollie often did. "So, do you think you will go back to live with your father after this?" Aarick wondered.

He really couldn't imagine that her father would want her going to Northland. Aarick knew that Pepper's father was never fond of her going to Northland in the first place.

Pepper shrugged as she cleaned a bottle for a potion. "Well, I won't know until I actually see him," Pepper stated. "There is just something that I feel I need to talk with him about. I just don't remember what it possibly is," Pepper lamented. Aarick knew there was something that clearly upset her. He put his hand on her shoulder and was about to say something when...

***

"Aarick, we need to get going before you are late for this parent/ principal meeting." Said a blonde girl who looked like a slightly younger and much blonder version of Pepper. "How am I supposed to pretend to be your parent if I am in class at the same time?" a slightly older-looking version of Aarick asked. They were in a living room that looked oddly familiar.

"I haven't thought everything through yet. I just know it will work out, though. It had better work out. I can't get suspended for something that Elle did," the girl said.

Another blonde girl that Aarick recognized from previous visions walked downstairs. She was dressed like an office manager who was going for drinks afterward.

"I am not responsible for you borrowing one of my erotic stories for a class assignment," the girl who Aarick assumed was Elle said. "Besides, I'm your English teacher. You realize I would see the damn thing at some point." She took out a cigarette, only it was a marijuana-based one.

The other girl stomped her foot, "You told me to cheat!" the blonde girl said. Elle rolled her eyes, "I told you to cheat. I didn't tell you to be messy about it," as she put her right hand on her hip. "Are we carpooling because I'm drunk?" The Elle woman asked out loud. His future self-rubbed his forehead, "You're drunk and about to teach honors English. Wonderful..." Aarick told her. "I'm sober enough, and it isn't English. It's chemistry," Elle explained.

His future self got a phone call before he could respond to that. "Hello... Mollie..., what do you mean you are somewhere in Japan? Well, figure... Mollie..., no, I cannot send money... I'll... no, do not call Sally. I'll figure it out. Ok. Ok! Goodbye," he said as he hung up the phone. He looked at the two girls, "She's doing great. Just great."

***

"I just had the weirdest vision of the future where I was talking with this blonde version of you," Aarick explained. Pepper looked at him. Something about this statement hit her rather hard. "My sister," Pepper said out of nowhere. Sister? Aarick was confused now, "Pepper, you don't have a sister." He thought for a moment, "Although, I've had visions of that girl before, and she really does look like you."

Pepper rubbed her eyes. She looked at him and started to frown, "It wasn't a dream. My mother came to me in some form of purgatory, which is weird considering we are Jewish. Regardless, she told me I had a twin sister who was sent several years into the future when we were both born to hide her from my grandmother. My own grandmother."

Pepper's eyes widened, "Grandmother Spellington is not a nice person." She stood up and started to walk around a little bit. Aarick got up himself and tried to comfort her, "Are you sure about this?" Pepper nodded, "I know it sounds a bit crazy, but it happened. It just had to have happened." After everything that had transpired, this was far from the most farfetched thing that Aarick had heard.

"Pepper, I believe you. I just don't know how you want to go about using this information," he explained to her. Pepper stopped walking and thought for a moment, "That's a very good point. I have no idea myself." It actually helped to know that again; he was alive in the future.

"I mean, do you want to find her? Clearly, I have some form of interaction with her in the future," he pointed out, which was true. So, they must have gone about looking for her at some point. "I mean, at some point, we must find her." He looked at her for a moment, "She really does look like you."

As the two continued to prep on their end, Sally walked downstairs with Mollie following her. Sally looked ready to go off on her older sister. Aarick had always sensed that Sally was not fond of how Mollie and Pepper treated her. He had always attempted to be nicer. Yet, he really couldn't control the way that Mollie or Pepper, for that matter, chose to act around her. "I'm not arguing with you, Mollie. You are going to stand in the crowd and not get hurt," the younger Magica sister screamed. Mollie huffed and puffed, "You and Pepper get to be involved in all of this! Why can't I?" she screamed as she plopped herself down on a stair step. Sally walked over to Aarick and looked as if to say that he needed to handle this.

Aarick sighed and got up, "Look, Mollie, you were a cat for how many years? I can't be worried about you while this is all going down. I need to be the bate. Sally will collect the blood sample, and Pepper is going to make it air bound. Do you have any other questions?" Mollie looked at him and shook her head no. "Look, we have a future. A weird one, but we have a future together. So, we should try to be as safe as possible," Aarick told all of them. He really hoped that Maude and Salloom would be alright on their end. Hope and reality were two different neighborhoods, though.

***

"Well, I could try it this way, but I know it won't work that way," Magisha screamed at herself. The door opened behind her. She quickly turned around, and she was in shock. However, she needed to play it cool. "Well, it took you long enough to come to your senses." Maude walked in.

"You look fatter," Magisha said as she walked over to her desk and sat down. "Where is Salloom? Is he holding out?" Maude just stood at the door. "No, he's dead set against ever seeing you again. He's actually in the streets below us trying to get protesters to side against you," Maude explained. Magisha nodded her head. That was typical Salloom. "Well, who needs him? He always comes back in the long run. We will be better without him for the moment," Magisha explained.

Maude looked her up and down. Magisha could easily tell that something was up. She had been around the block enough times to tell. "Ok, what's wrong?" the Queen asked. Maude sighed, "Well, this is a wreck." Maude walked closer to her as she looked her in the eye, "You can't possibly tell me that you are ok with this. Hallowton is on fire. The Magic Realm is on fire. You have Humans trying to break down portals so they can rob us of non-existent natural resources!" her secretary screamed at her.

Typical Maude going off on her. Nothing out of the ordinary. She was used to it at this point. "Are you done ranting?" she asked her. Magisha got up again and attempted to look out her window. She realized it was too high up. "You're back. I'm willing to be generous. You can stay, but I'm going to have to cut your pay. You did leave without notice," Magisha explained. Maude scoffed at this. Magisha turned around, "Do I sense an attitude? Do you really think that is appropriate given all you put me through?" Magisha screamed.

Maude laughed, "I'm not here to make amends. I'm here as a final plea to you. You've lost your mind. You've lost any drive you may have had. For what? What exactly do you want with Aarick? Is killing a child really going to make things better, Magisha?" Maude demanded to know. Magisha was sick of this accusation, "I am not trying to kill Aarick. I am trying to remold him into what he always should have been."

Maude looked on both sides of her as if there were people there. "You had the option! Ryder and Evangelista are the worst parents on this earth. That boy hasn't seen his mother since he was ten years old. His father only cares about his well-being for a merger. You could have had him at any point. He adored you!" Maude screamed at the top of her lungs. Once again, nobody ever listened to Magisha, and it was starting to become offensive. "I don't want him to have the option to go back to his old life. He is supposed to be the son that I never got to raise!" Magisha said as if Maude, in her current state, actually knew what she was talking about.

Maude once again looked at her flabbergasted, "What son? You've never taken an interest in the children you do have! The only child you ever raised was Gem, and even then, Salloom and I got to be the ones who were there for her while you did weird things," Maude retorted.

Magisha couldn't believe the way she was being spoken to, "I already kicked Gem out of here. I'll tell you the same thing I told her. I just won't see you ever again," Magisha said as a threat. "You're going to have to do better than that," Maude spat out. She walked over to the couch and sat down herself.

"I said you can leave," Magisha said. "Ok, after you pay me retribution for the centuries of nonsense that you put me through while you obsessed over a boy that is not yours," Maude screamed! A part of Magisha wanted to throw Maude through the window. "Come on, pay up," Maude said as she made little gestures with her hands.

Magisha was past her last nerve and started to hover over to Maude, "This is rich... You waltz back in here and start to make demands? I'll kill you. I don't need Magic to kill you," the Queen threatened. "You could kill me. Only one issue," Maude put her hand on her cheek. "I know where Aarick is. You don't. I'm the only person in the entire world that knows his location. Salloom doesn't even know his location," Maude gloated.

***

"All closets double as elevators!" screamed Aarick as he fell out of his Northland closet. His room was as he had left it. Mollie, Pepper, and Sally all followed behind him, and they all had the same look on their faces. "It's all the same," Sally said out loud. "You would have assumed that Magisha would have gone looking for clues or something or that people looking for you would have tried to break in," Pepper added.

Aarick sat on his bed. He forgot how uncomfortable of a bed it was, and sadly it was a replacement mattress from the one that had been in the room. He could see his reflection in the mirror. He had seen himself a few times over the past few days, but this was the first time he had really taken a moment to grasp things. He had grown several inches. He was thinner than he had ever been. A lot paler, and he had a natural tan about him usually. It was so surreal. It was disturbing to see. He was no longer Aarick Langston. He wasn't sure what he was.

"Ok, Pepper and Sally, you need to stick together. You need to go the way that Maude plotted out for you. Do not use the main staircase at the Capital Building to get upstairs. When I appear in time square you need to be hiding in her office," he said as he looked at them, hoping that they would listen. They both had these fake smiles on their faces. This was a hopeless plan. The two girls were never going to work together, but he had to trust that at the very least Pepper would be able to get the antidote airborne.

"We will see each other soon," Sally said. Pepper hugged him goodbye, but Sally only gave one last glance. "We really need to go about redoing this room when school starts back up," Mollie said nervously.

Aarick sighed, "Mollie, there is a chance that we won't be going to this school. If my visions are true, then I know we don't go here in the future for certain. I had a vision earlier where I received a call from you asking for money while you were off somewhere," Aarick explained.

Mollie gulped and sat down on the bed. "I just got you back though." She explained. This made him feel guilty. "Like I said... You were calling me." Aarick could tell that this upset her. "Mollie... There are no other girls that will ever best you or Pepper in my life. You do realize that?" He was speaking from his heart. "Our days as Northland Royalty are probably over though." He put his hand on her shoulder.

Mollie gulped and sat down on the bed, "I just got you back, though," she explained. This made him feel guilty, "As I said, you were calling me."

Aarick could tell that this upset her, "Mollie, there are no other girls who will ever top you or Pepper in my life. You do realize that?" he asked, as he spoke from his heart. "Our days as Northland Royalty are probably over." He put his hand on her shoulder.

Mollie stood up and got herself together, "Please be careful." She gave him a very tight hug. She looked him in the eye, "I mean it. I don't care what your visions say. You are my best friend, Aarick. You can't leave me alone with Pepper and the rest of the world." He kissed her on the forehead, "If I can survive this, then I promise you Molina M. Magica, that I will never leave you." She smiled at this, "Good," the Blonde Witch responded.

CHAPTER EIGHTEEN

THE END OF THIS

"**I** beg you, people, to listen to me before it is too late!" screamed Salloom at the top of his lungs from the steps of the Capital Building. "You need to understand that the Queen, my ex-wife, is not right in the head. Aaron-Richard is not the enemy. Our own Queen has turned on us," he begged and pleaded with this crowd.

He had been attempting to get them to listen for over an hour now. It was not working out very well. He had already seen Pepper and Sally run through the crowd. Aarick would not be long now. He just needed to keep this crowd going for a few moments longer. "You don't need a Queen. You need the lives you had back, that you had before this mess!" he screamed. "Come on Aarick. It's time."

This crowd was made up of anti-Magisha and pro-Magisha people and people who were just angry at the universe at this point. Salloom understood where most were coming from. He was just as big of a victim of Magisha as everyone in this crowd. If anything, he was the biggest victim of all. He needed to get out of his head before he himself burned the Capital Building down.

"You can all stop arguing. I've decided to confront her myself." Screamed a voice so loud that you could hear it in the Human Realm. The crowd turned around, and people gathered from wherever they were. Aarick walked out from the front gate of Northland. He was wearing his Northland uniform. It was a little bit extra, but Salloom thought it was on par with something Magisha probably would have done.

"The boy!" screamed someone from the crowd. More people started to scream similar things. "Get him!" another person said. People started to run towards him. Aarick didn't flinch. He put his hands in the air. The crowd was pushed back as a force shield formed around him.

"Don't make me laugh," Aarick said as he walked forward. The people in the crowd were trying to break down at this point. Salloom could sense that even some of the anti-Magisha people were turning now. He supposed that it could have had something to do with the fact that they never thought this would end until this point. Yet, here they were standing so close to Aarick Langston.

"MAGISHA STONE! GET DOWN HERE AND FIGHT ME!" the Langston boy screamed.

***

It was all show. Aarick was terrified. It was far from the first time that he was putting on a show. He just hoped it was good enough to throw Magisha off a bit. "Come on, get down here!"

She had to have known he was here by now. What was taking so long? "Come..." he didn't have time to finish. A giant cloud of black smoke appeared in time square. People ran for a distance. "Well, it took you long enough." She screamed.

He had seen her briefly the other day but not long enough to really notice her current state. She looked awful. She really did. She looked as if she hadn't slept in years. Her hair was a mess. Her outfit was unkempt. It didn't look like she was wearing any makeup. Aarick was terrified, not for his life, but for the shape she was in. It was sad, but he still cared about her. She needed to be stopped, and it might not end well for her, but this needed to end. If only for the people in the crowd and not for either of them. This wasn't fair anymore to anyone. "Lower your shield," the Queen demanded as she put her hands on her hips. "I won't hurt you. At least not yet." She explained.

Aarick looked over at Salloom. Magisha turned to see what he was looking at, "Oh, what a pity. You're still alive, I see," Magisha said. She turned back around. "We can do this in one of two ways. We can battle it out, and you know I will win. If you think I don't know how to break a force shield, you are nuts." The Queen explained.

Aarick kept looking at Salloom for some form of advice on what to do next. Magisha started to laugh, "Aaron-Richard, stop looking at him! He doesn't have the answers. If he had the answers, this would have been over long ago. You've known me your entire life. I always get what I want. I don't stand down until I get what I want," the Queen told him.

He lowered the shield. Aarick knew very well that Sally and Pepper were close, if not already in place by now. Magisha walked close to him. She formed a ball of fire in her hand. The look on her face was now disturbing. He tried to back up but knew that he needed to form another shield, but he was too nervous. "What the heck?" she screamed. Her hand was frozen. "Don't even think about it!" screamed a familiar voice, a familiar blonde voice.

Magisha started to look around, "Where is that girl? Are you still a cat? Everyone look for a cat or a pretty blonde girl." Aarick didn't see her anywhere, though. Mollie was doing what she was told. She was blending in with the crowd. Aarick had to say he was proud of her for listening for once.

Her hand dethawed. She didn't reform the ball of fire. Instead, she grabbed onto Aarick's wrist, "Alright, anyone who tries to harm me now will accidentally hurt the boy. I'm taking him to my office to deal with him there," Magisha stated to everyone. He felt that the only person she was actually speaking to was him, though. Aarick closed his eyes, and when he opened them again, he was in her office. It was an absolute mess and smelled like cat urine, which he really didn't want to put two and two together on.

"Well... I think you and I can agree this has gone on for long enough. Why don't you just accept defeat?" Magisha stated. She was speaking extremely manic. Maude was sitting on the couch and looked frozen, but she wasn't. She was scared. "I don't hate you. I just want what you can become. I want to teach you. I need to teach you," Magisha explained.

Aarick stomped his foot on the ground, "Teach me what? Why couldn't you have come to me with your problems when you were angry? No, you couldn't because you had to make yourself believe that you were right, and if I told you no or had an excuse, then you would have claimed I was being unreasonable," Aarick screamed at her. He was sick of this. He got right in her face. "You don't want to help me. You don't want to help the people down there." He pointed to the window. "You want it your way and only your way. I have no idea what I've done that isn't up to your standard. It must be a lot, though. Do you want to know what? Do you really want to know? I don't care. I'm Aaron-Richard Mitchel Langston. I'm untouchable. Even more now than before. You could never find me. I had to come to you. So, tough luck, lady. You've already lost."

She was fuming. Aarick looked and saw Sally from behind her. She had a small knife and a glass. She poked her in the arm. "What the heck?" Magisha screamed. She turned around. "The younger Magica girl? What are you doing here?" Magisha screamed. Sally looked furious, "The younger Magica girl? My name is Sally. Salina Loretta Magica. Learn the name," Sally said as if she was a grown adult demanding respect. She then made a run for it.

Magisha turned back to Aarick, "What did... I don't care," as she put her hand on Aarick's throat. "If you don't want to listen to me, then I'll just kill you." She explained.

Aarick tried to form a force shield. He tried to think up a spell that he could cast, but he had to admit it; he was just too weak after all this time. The thing was that she was weak too. Sally got the blood. Pepper would be able to make it air bound. As Aarick started to fall to the ground, the glass from her window broke. In came Mollie and Salloom riding on a familiar pink dragon. "Ainsley!" screamed Sally. Maude finally got up from the couch, "We are not keeping her!" screamed Maude.

Magisha let go of Aarick. Salloom was getting weak again. Aarick could see Pepper in the lobby mixing things together. They needed to hurry up before Magisha started to figure out what was going on.

"Hurry!" Aarick screamed as loud as he could, even with his neck now being sore. Aarick needed to do something. Magisha was clearly about to create another ball of fire or something. This was all too much. He didn't ask to be born rich. He didn't ask to be born male. Aarick didn't ask for the ability to have premonitions. The Langston child didn't ask to be a Witch, for that matter. He was sick of this. He stood as tall as he could and just yelled, "I just want you to STOP!"

As he said that, the room went very still. Everyone around him was frozen. "Hello?" he said out loud. Magisha was frozen in time. Everyone else was as well. Maude, of course, was frozen, scratching herself, but that just seemed typical. He had no idea how long this would last, but he had an idea. The teenage Witch quickly walked over to Mollie.

Aarick took a deep breath, hoping that this would work. "Unfreeze," he said. He closed his eyes. "What's going on?" Mollie asked. Aarick opened his eyes in relief. Mollie was the only one other than him who was moving. "Ok, quickly, freeze Magisha in a deep frost." Aarick told her. Mollie looked mortified. "What are you talking about? It would kill her." Mollie pointed out. "I need you to focus. Her entire body is frozen. I need you to create a layer that is so cold that she cannot move from it. Can you do that?" he asked her.

It was then he had an even more brilliant idea. He ran into the lobby and unfroze Pepper. "What on earth?" she screamed. "I need you to turn Magisha into a liquid state," he explained. This was it; it was now or never. If he could get Pepper to turn her into a liquid puddle while her mind and body were still frozen in time, then Mollie could safely freeze her without killing her. She, however, wouldn't be able to turn herself back into a solid state. The three of them concentrated.

"On the count of three!" Aarick shouted. "One... two... three...," they all said. At that moment, time around them started to move again, except for Magisha, who was still standing in place. Pepper turned her into a fluid state. It was as if the Wicked Witch was melting. Mollie then froze her beyond reason.

Sally ran over to the now block of ice along with Salloom and Maude. Salloom looked at Maude and then Aarick. "You, did it?" he said. "She's actually stopped."

Salloom looked melancholy but also more than relieved. Aarick wanted to celebrate but then realized that they had to get the Gray Stone reversed. "Ok, Pepper, we need to get this air born." Pepper ran back into the lobby but then walked back in, "It's missing!" She screamed.

Aarick rubbed his forehead. Why did this shock him? Of course, it went missing. Then a cloud of white smoke appeared. "We will take care of that." Three people appeared from the cloud of smoke. They were all wearing white robes: two men and a woman. Maude stomped over to them, "Aren't you a little late?" She clearly knew them.

"We are always on time," the lone female stated.

Aarick had a weird feeling he knew who they were. "Are you the Council of Three?" he asked. Sally dropped her jaw at the statement.

"We are," they all said in unison. The younger of the two men stood forward, "We are finally ready to step in and fix all of this. Thank you for your services." Thank you for your services? Were they on drugs? Aarick had just spent the last few years being kidnapped, brainwashed, and having his childhood ripped out from him. These three idiots wanted to appear out of nowhere to fix things now?

"Did you always have the ability to fix things?" Aarick demanded. The woman now stepped forward, "Yes. The Council of Three, even in past versions, have wanted to remove Magisha. We have been working with fortune-tellers and seers to figure out the best time to finally strike. We've been watching closely for the last fourteen years for this particular moment. It was the only way," the woman explained.

"Maybe you can step in, but you can't get the Magic Realm to agree with you. That's why it exists in the first place." Maude shouted at them. Aarick could tell that she was just as mad, if not more. "We won't let you take control of this situation," Salloom explained. The older of the two men now stepped forward, "It is rather simple. You are the multi-time ex-husband. Maude is the best friend. Every child in this room has a long-rooted family friendship with the now defeated Queen. No one in the Realm can take over as an ultimate ruler. We are not ridding the Universe of the Magic Realm. We are just taking control of it once and for all. It was a bold experiment, but it failed," the Councilman explained.

The woman held the antidote, "I will replicate this and cause a storm that will be last long enough that the cure will touch everyone within three days. We will fix the damage done to the Human Realm at that time. All Humans will forget everything. Then, we will announce the new status quo amongst the Magic Realm," she told them all. Aarick wanted to continue, but they snapped their fingers and were gone before he could.

CHAPTER NINETEEN

IT'S OVER, ISN'T IT?

It had been over a week, and the Council of Three had fixed everything and taken credit for it. People were not sure how to react towards the capture of Magisha. Aarick had no idea where her remains were. The Council of Three had stolen those along with the antidote. Maude had explained that several other things had gone missing as well but had not given any detail. "Come in," Aarick said. "I didn't even knock yet," Sally explained as she opened his bedroom door. He had been having much more clear visions as of late. It felt like his powers were in overload for the past few weeks. Salloom pointed out that being on a binding potion for three years had not helped the situation.

"Well... I don't know," Aarick told her. "I thought you were staying at home?" Aarick asked her. He had been staying in his dorm room even though Northland was shut down at this time. There were rumors that it might open again in the Fall. The only reason he was staying there was that he hadn't been able to sleep in his room at his house. It wasn't his room. Sally and Mollie went back to their mother's home.

"Well, I am, but I needed to speak with you alone," Sally said as she walked over to his bed and sat down next to him. "This isn't fair."

He didn't disagree, but at the end of the day, "A lot of things aren't fair, Sally. We just have to live with it." There were rumors that Magisha would be partially unfrozen and put on trial. There were other rumors that she would be turned to Stone and put next to Merlin for the rest of forever. The Witches of the Magic Realm were not ok with the Council of Three taking over. There was talk of going after them. It was all talk, though. These Witches allowed Magisha to terrorize for centuries.

"Mollie mentioned a day school in the next town over. Do you think you will go with her?" Aarick asked. Sally buried herself into a pillow, "I very much doubt it." She looked up, "I also kind of doubt that Mollie will start going to class. It would be much more difficult for them to get away with things at school than before, because Magisha let them all act out without punishment. They both laughed. "Have you heard from Gem?" she asked. Aarick hadn't, which scared him. Maude said that she had high hopes she was perfectly fine. It was probably for the best that she stayed in hiding for a while, if at all possible. People wanted her to be the scapegoat for all of this. Magisha's children all withdrew from the conversation when asked about it by the press. They were not going to take any credit, which they shouldn't. It wasn't like they played a part.

"Pepper will be around to visit later today," Aarick explained. It was so weird not to have Mollie and Pepper on the other end of the building. It was weird not to have anyone else in the building, aside from Maude, who had been staying in his guest room. "Are we all still having dinner tonight?" Sally asked. As far as Aarick knew they were.

***

"I think that this is ridiculous. They are giving me an hour to decide what I want and what I don't want, and even then, I don't necessarily get to keep it," Maude spat out as Salloom helped her clean out her desk. "Where am I supposed to live? I can't stay in that dorm room forever, and I'm not moving back into my house," Maude explained to him. "I mean, I guess you could go back to the house in Australia," Salloom pointed out.

Maude sat down at her desk, "I considered it for a brief moment but apparently, as part of the fixing, the Council of Three removed it from exitance!" As she pounded her fist on the desk.

Years and years of memories, even if they were tainted by what Magisha had become, were going to be lost forever because power-hungry Human Realm Witches wanted to be in charge. It wasn't that she expected to stick around. "I don't even know what I want yet. What are you going to do?" she asked.

Salloom turned and looked away, "I'm going to move back to England. I want to set up a small lab and just sort of work on things that actually interest me. This will be the first time in my life where Magisha won't be involved. I need to accept that my children are never going to forgive me for the things that she caused." It was then that Maude remembered something important, "Magisha said something about Aarick. She said that he was her son."

Salloom immediately turned back and looked at her. She could tell that this didn't sit well with him. "That's impossible. She would never have slept with Ryder Langston. Ryder would never have been able to keep quiet about that. Plus, we all saw Evangelista pregnant with him." Salloom pointed out. These were all excellent points, yet Maude had to wonder, "I mean... maybe she meant it in the sense that she cared about him like son. It's not like she even raised her own children. That may be what she meant. I guess," Maude said as she wanted to make total sense of it. Magisha wouldn't have tried to kill her own son. Would she have?

"We can never tell Aarick. You do realize that, right?" Salloom asked her. Maude nodded in agreement, "Oh, I have no intention. I don't want to even plant that seed." Maude then thought for a moment longer, "The citizens of the Realm will never allow for The Council of Three to be in charge. How long do we think this will last?" she asked him.

Salloom shrugged, "Honestly, Maude, at this point, I don't care. I understand why Aarick and the kids and you are all upset over this. You just have to understand that for me; I'm free. I think over time you will get it as well," Salloom explained. Maude understood where he was coming from. "We can't leave Aarick alone after this," Maude noted.

"I have no intention. He will always have access to me. I hate saying this because you know how much I'm not a fan of the Langston family, but the best thing for Aarick is to just be a Langston. He will probably transfer to Orion Oakland. He will marry and join the other Langston's and just be infamous like the rest of his family." The ex-teacher theorized.

Maude didn't like this at all. She wanted Aarick in her life. She wanted the Aarick that she had gotten to know, the one who only had the Langston name on the surface. "I fear this battle isn't over. Magisha never accepts defeat. She's not dead," Maude reminded him. Salloom shrugged, "She might not be, but I fear that the Council of Three is not going to let her have power again. They have just been waiting for her to snap publicly. The Magic Realm might not accept them as their new leader, but a decent amount of them grasps the fact that Magisha shouldn't be in-charge anymore. I fear for how they choose to handle this," Salloom told her.

***

"Pepper, your grandmother will be here soon," her father explained. Pepper smiled but felt off for some reason. Something about her grandmother felt off, but she couldn't figure out why. It had been so long since she had been home. This was the most time she had spent with her father in years. "When will I be going back to school?" Pepper asked David Spellington. David looked at her, a bit taken back, "Pepper, sweety, you just got out of a coma and helped save the world. Do you really feel the need to go back to school right this moment?"

Pepper frowned. Her father really didn't get her at all, which was rather annoying. "I just miss my friends," Pepper admitted to David. David picked up an old book of Pepper's. He read the title and put it down, "Well, the Langston and Magica families are not exactly the best of people. Your mother had some peculiar friends. The Kensington's too. I don't know who is worse, Ryder Langston, Octavia Kensington..." David shook his head in disbelief.

The Spellington girl had yet to inform her father that she had a secret twin sister. She wasn't exactly sure how to explain that to him. Her mother, Penelope, had passed on years ago, and she had a feeling that David would not understand. "I intend to stay friends with Aarick Langston." She would reluctantly stay in contact with Mollie Magica if it were that important to Aarick. David sighed, "I can't force you to stay away from him, but I'd prefer that you not return to school in the Magic Realm. I can find you a new school here."

The absurdity. Pepper would have loved to have heard this when she was ten but at fourteen years old? No. It was too late. David was her father, and she truly loved him, but he had spent years keeping them apart. She didn't know why. All she knew was that she had a secret twin sister but was still foggy on why the twin was secret.

"Why don't you take a semester off?" David suggested as he walked towards her door. "You are already grades ahead of the people around you. Why would you want less?" David said. He blew her a kiss as he left the room and closed the door. Pepper was left alone with her thoughts, "I'm grades ahead of a lot of people," she said under her breath. She grabbed a backpack.

***

Life was back to normal, in the sense that Magisha was no longer chasing after them. Aarick had to admit that he was relieved. Yet, things were not back to normal. They were also not how the vision had played out in his head. Obviously, that must have come later. He just wanted it to come now. Even if it was clear that it wasn't at Northland, he had received an email earlier that Northland would stay open through alumni. He somehow didn't feel this new version of Northland would be as welcoming to him. Yet, he didn't really want to leave it either.

Aarick walked out onto the Northland courtyard and sat on a familiar bench. Pepper orbed into an open space next to him a few moments later. "I'm not in the Human Realm. At least not without you," the redhead explained. Aarick was about to speak when a blonde figure wearing all pink walked over and sat down on the other side of him.

"My mother tried to enroll me into the new school today. Yeah, I don't think so. That said, I got an attachment email from the Northland alumni group. They don't want me back because of my GPA," Mollie buried her head in her lap. "I've spoken to my idiot nanny. My father sends his regards. My mother has said nothing. One of my sisters said 'Hi' to me in passing, just 'Hi'," Aarick said, glancing forward.

The three started to laugh. "We may never go to school together again. We may never be the supposedly popular kids ever again. That all said, you two will always be in my life. I don't care how much the two of you personally can't stand each other. You are my forever people," Aarick explained to them.

He waited for one of them to say something and the other to scream something. Instead, they both hugged him. "We should probably get going to the restaurant." Pepper explained. She stood up.

They were about to walk away when a familiar and unwanted

figure blinked in. "I have a proposition for you three." Smythe said. Aarick started to form a force shield. "No need to protect yourselves." Smythe explained. Aarick looked at Pepper and Mollie, who both looked equally as confused as he felt, "What do you possibly want?" Aarick asked.

Smythe laughed, "As I said. I have a proposition for you. The three of you were royally screwed over by the Council of Three. They aren't done with you. I can promise you that." Smythe told them. Aarick didn't need to hear this, "Yeah, well... screw them, screw you." He shrugged. "We can all help each other," Smythe explained. Pepper now got in front, "You work for a terrorist organization. Why on earth would we agree to work with you?" the red-haired Witch asked. This once again caused Smythe to laugh, "The WIA is not a terrorist organization. It's a group against creating high Archy amongst powerful people." Their former Dean told them.

Aarick now mistrusted Royalty and the people in power. However, that didn't change the fact that the WIA felt the need to kidnap him and Sally. It was also obvious that they knew of Magisha's plans before anyone else, which made him question what else they knew. "You know things about the Council of Three? Don't you?" The Teenage Witch asked. Smythe nodded, "A great deal. Let's put it this way; there are certain things that they have not told you, in particular, Aarick. Things that my Boss is aware of." Smythe told them.

This was intriguing, but it wasn't enough for him to just agree to anything. "No. I'm not interested," he said as he looked at Pepper and Mollie. They both nodded in agreement. They started to walk away. Smythe did not follow them. At least not to their knowledge.

Aarick took a deep breath as they walked out the front gates, "I'm going to take a short walk by myself." Aarick stated. He was out of breath a bit. Pepper nodded, "We will meet you there then." She took Mollie's hand, and they walked off.

Aarick looked around. It was getting dark out. This was ridiculous. The sad thing was that he actually believed Smythe. It made sense. The Council of Three probably did know certain things. The WIA probably did as well. What? He could only imagine, but honestly, he didn't want to. Aarick looked at the Capital Building and looked up. He needed to do something.

***

It took half an hour to get up the staircase. He walked into the lobby of Magisha's office. It had already been stripped down from what it used to look like. The teen had no clue what they planned to do with it. It would make sense that a power-hungry individual would want to claim the office for themselves. Personally, he would find it sick for someone to want to work in here. He pushed open the door and walked into Magisha's office. It, too, had been cleaned out. The desk was still there, and that was it.

"Well, it's over," Aarick said. He closed his eyes for a moment. "Yes. It is," A voice that terrorized him said. He quickly opened his eyes, and Magisha was standing behind him. "What on earth? How did you? Where did you... Why are you here?" Aarick asked.

The Queen looked insane. Truly insane. She was wearing a blue gown with one of her crowns. Yet, she was so much thinner and paler than her former self. Aarick started to back away from her towards the desk. "Please leave me alone. I don't know what you want," Aarick said, truly frightened. She kept walking forward, "I renounce my Magical abilities. I renounce my Magical abilities. I renounce my Magical abilities!" she said three times, each time getting louder and louder.

The window was still broken, and a gust of wind rushed into the room. A blue light formed around Magisha's skin that quickly escaped her. She pushed Aarick aside, "I was wrong. You win. Have fun being King. It's what you always wanted."

She was standing with her back against the open hole in the wall and smiled. Magisha took one final step back and fell. She didn't scream. She smiled, "It's finally over," the Queen said as her body drifted away in the distance. Aarick dropped to his knees and looked down. He could no longer see her. If what she had just said was true, she no longer was Magical or Immortal. "She just killed herself." Aarick whispered to himself. She's gone. She just said he could finally be King? He had no idea what that meant. "Well... that was vicious..."

ACKNOWLEDGEMENTS

Attached to this novel is 23-years of people, places, and things. Eleven homes, nine schools, four post high school day jobs... Love, loss, etc... *Technically Magic* existed in some way shape or form.

This novel wouldn't exist in its published form without the help of my artist luviiilove who created the most current renditions of all of the characters. Thank you luviii for a five-year collaboration that I will never forget. I wish you all the luck going forward. I also thank my new artist Milkaela for stepping in to draw a rendition of the character of Sally.

I give a round of applause to my editor Sandra Watts for always going above and beyond. It means the world to me as my learning disability dysgraphia makes it difficult to properly punctuate on my own. I also thank polyarts36 for the incredible work they have done with formatting the pages and cover of the book. A similar shoutout and thank you to my video team vwebbs123 who have created video ads throughout 2021.

People have come and gone... Nikki Baker has remained the first person I share art renditions with, the first person I pitch ideas too, and the first person who I seek criticism from. I wouldn't have it any other way through probably eight drafts (I wish I was joking).

Josh Patterson. I don't think I could ask for a better best friend. You've helped push and motivate me. You help humble me (whether I like it or not). Love you always.

My favorite Welsh boy... Ryan thank you for your kindness, your perspectives, and just being a person, I have been able to turn to through the final part of this crazy journey. You're an incredible human being. More than anything.

Sue Ann Facey. One of my greatest supporters. It means the world to me. Thank you for standing with me in more ways than one.

Devona and Lark... Thank you for getting me through one of the most bizarre Journy's I had ever taken in order to publish novels. You both are forever a part of my legacy and am honored to still have you in my lives even if from a distance.

Carol Roth my business idol, Buff Faye my queen, and Milos my doll bestie thank you all for the genuine intrigue and support on your ends in differing ways. It means the world.

Alexander and Manny my brothers... You both have existed through the versions of this story. You both are the only two who can share some of the trivial situations attached to the memories that some of the scenes within the novel have countered. Very much and more than anything.

Thank you to my parents Ralph and Lisa Marie. Through every sport I quit, every after-school activity I grew tired of, every a-typical situation you supported me.

Finally for my readers. Whether you have read my previous work or this is your first novel you have read of mine. Thank you. Thank you. Thank you!

ABOUT THE AUTHOR

L A Michaels (He/ Him) is a Michigan-born and raised author who also lived in Kansas and South Carolina while in high school. L A worked for the TVMegaSite for over ten years, writing recaps and summaries for daytime TV. L A is also the author of the "Between Heaven and Hell" series as well as the novel "I Love You, I Hate You, I Miss You." When L A is not writing, he watches theatre, drag, old movies, and reading comics or reading other books himself.

Twitter: lamichaels1995

Instagram: lamichaelsauthor

Facebook: L A Michaels

Goodreads: L A Michaels

Follow my artist Luviiilove on their DeviantArt account of the same name! Checkout my new artist Milkaela on Instagram @_milkaela.